# Sniffing Out Scandal

## LAYERS OF MYSTERY
### BOOK THREE

## LEANNE BAKER

CKN Christian Publishing
An Imprint of Wolfpack Publishing
9850 S. Maryland Parkway, Suite A-5 #323
Las Vegas, Nevada 89183

cknchristianpublishing.com

Print ISBN 978-1-63977-999-4
eBook ISBN 978-1-63977-989-5
LCCN 2022951421

# Sniffing Out Scandal

# Chapter One

I couldn't help but get a bit choked up as the salesperson drove my trusty Camry away. That car had helped keep my sanity during the most miserable time of my life. I'd logged a lot of miles behind the wheel of that dependable, comfortable vehicle. I'd come to rely on it as one of the few things I could count on in my chaotic life. It worked well for Southern California highway miles, and even in the summer, it was fine in my hometown of Bishop.

Last May, I'd suffered the last straw and ended my ten-year marriage with little more in my pocket than my paid-for Camry. It had become a symbol of the new freedom I hoped to live. And it served me well through the summer. But now, with autumn turning the leaves to the vibrant end of summer colors, I would need something with a four-wheel drive in my mountain home.

Bishop, California, didn't often get enough snow to justify buying an SUV, but I'd been exploring my hometown area after being gone for a decade. Bishop is known as the small town with a big backyard. A yard without artificial boundaries. From the Sierra Nevada Mountain Range to the west and Nevada's White Mountains to the east, Bishop is nestled in the Owens Valley. The natural attractions of the mountains, canyons, and the high desert are unique and enthralling. From elevations of seven thousand feet over Bishop's elevation of forty-one hundred and fifty feet, there was much to see and experience. Even growing up here, I hadn't seen it all. There was still much to explore.

And my partner in crime required a bit more space. Rusty was a rescued golden retriever and Irish Setter mix who loved to roam. He was the perfect companion for my mountain hikes. The new car was a silver 2021 Subaru Forester all-wheel drive SUV that wasn't really new. I'd bought it from a dealership in town that'd purchased a fleet of one-year-old rental cars. No matter. It was new enough for me.

As I got behind the wheel, the two-tone brown interior features overwhelmed me. The Camry was ten years old and didn't have a lot of luxuries. This vehicle did. Inside, a ten-inch information and entertainment display dominated the top of the console area. Below was a push-button ignition which I particularly liked as well as a push-button transmission. I wasn't sure about changing gears, but I'd get used to it. The ergonomic seats were comfortable for my long legs to reach the steering wheel and console. Visibility to the outside was excellent. The new car smell was long gone, but I could tell the car had been thoroughly cleaned. That was good enough.

I pushed the button for the back hatch to open and got out. This would be Rusty's quarters. Loading a weed and sticker-laden, muddy pooch in the back was much more satisfactory than putting him in the Camry's passenger seat. I stood directly behind the liftgate, and seconds later, it raised to full open.

Yes, this was a good choice.

So deep was my reverie about this new vehicle that when Oliver Driscoll strolled up beside me, I jumped.

"Oh, hi, Sarah. I haven't seen you in a while." Mom and Dad's balding, paunchy neighbor had worked in the accounting department at the dealership for as long as I could remember. He was the guy who'd run out from his office if he saw someone he knew on the off chance that he could impress. He wore typical Bishop business attire of his generation: a white button-up shirt with pearled buttons, Western-style polyester slacks, black-and-red cowboy boots, and a summer Stetson. If I'd seen him coming, I would've walked across the street.

But I hadn't, and I couldn't be rude to him as I saw him almost daily. I could usually keep it to a waving distance. But not today. He clasped his hands together, savoring something not apparent to me. I'd already bought a car from his dealership. I wouldn't be a sale tick on his score sheet.

The "Jingle Bell Rock" played obnoxiously over the dealership's PA system. I'd best be civil. "Hi, Oliver. Nice day, isn't it?" I looked around, hoping to find someone to distract him.

"It's gonna be cold, mark my words."

A stunning new pearled-white Lincoln Navigator pulled out from the detail shed. Now idling in the dealership's adjacent lot, it was a vehicle that commanded attention, as much for the style and color as the rarity of seeing a flashy Lincoln in Bishop. A vaguely familiar figure wrestled his way into the driver's seat. He was a man of Oliver's age, early sixties, and same medium height, but with curly salt-and-pepper hair grown a little past the monthly haircut.

"Who's that?" I asked, more to myself than to Oliver.

He heard and gave me an eager answer. "Oh, that's Norman Escher. Own's the coin shop on East Line Street."

Ah, Escher. His daughter rode high-school rodeo with my cousin Melody and me. I couldn't remember her name. She probably couldn't remember mine either. "Who knew coin collecting was so lucrative." If I remembered right, he used to drive an old blue Celica. His store was right next to Layers, the bakery I managed.

"No kidding. Do you know that model retails for over a hundred grand? And that paint job costs extra."

He got my attention. I was irritated by his ingratiating personality in the first place, but I found telling clients the price of other customers' cars marched close to crossing a line. "Oliver, do you report prices for all clients' cars to others? I sure hope I don't hear any repercussions about buying a used car." I pointed to my Subaru. "That sounds a bit unethical, although it could be just totally wrong."

"Really, Sarah." Oliver sputtered as the blush deepened on his face. "I was just trying to be sociable."

I pushed the button on the liftgate and watched it close. "Time to get back to work, Oliver." I couldn't say it was good to see him because it wasn't. "Until next time."

His full lips pursed under the ten-gallon Stetson. He whirled and strutted back into his air-conditioned showroom office.

❀

As I pulled into the employee parking space at Layers Bakery, something niggled at me. High Sierra Coins and Collectibles was next door, just across the alley from Layers. The parking spaces allocated to his business were empty. The closed sign hung on the door.

I had to let it go. It was none of my business. Maybe he had a client from whom he made a significant commission. I shrugged at my own nosiness and went to get Rusty to show him his new ride.

# Chapter Two

After a short look-see, I had to practically drag Rusty from the back of the Subaru when it was time to go back to work. He loved it, especially the room to lie down. I knew I'd have no trouble getting him back in the car when we went for hikes.

With the Subaru picked up, it was time to tackle the Christmas Fair. Because I'd done such a great job on the Fall Colors Festival, the chamber of commerce tapped me to head up the newly reorganized Christmas Fair. It was more likely that all the other capable leaders had run faster than me. In any event, I was in charge, and as I hadn't attended any of the events in the past ten years, I would have to reinvent the wheel.

Layers Bakery had recently taken a loan to remodel the front space of the store. My cousin, the original owner, had talked of opening a café in the front space. After her untimely death, I committed to her husband to manage the shop and construction until my own job as a court reporter opened in January.

The sawdust was swept up last night before the work

crew left, so everything looked in order. I'd been lucky enough to find the right contractor who would work after the bakery closed at three o'clock. Just to be sure, I called him.

"Van? It's Sarah Murray from Layers Bakery."

"Sarah, I'm glad you called. I wanted to ask you something."

"Sure."

"For the overhead lighting, did you want ten or twelve cans?"

I considered the price and the value for the extra cost. The room was light enough during the day, and we opened at six thirty when it was close to sunrise in the winter. I didn't want to skimp at this stage. "Twelve should give us all the light we need in the winter."

I heard him scratching a note.

"Is that all? Is everything else going okay?" I crossed my fingers.

"Yeah, it's all going fine. Looks like we'll be done by next week."

"Excellent. Just in time to put up Christmas decorations."

I heard the smile in his voice when he said goodbye.

The head baker, Libby, checked the trays in the proofing oven. She whirled around to flash a huge smile at me. It was almost noon, and I figured she was going to squeeze in a lunch.

"Sarah." I had wondered if marriage would make any difference in my friend and co-worker's appearance. Two months into wedded bliss, it hadn't. She still had purple hair, trimmed short on one side and long on the other. Her ear tunnels looked even bigger. "How about lunch?" She made quite the contrast with her cowboy husband.

"I've got to get moving on the Christmas Fair. Too much to do."

There was a gleam in her huge blue eyes that made me pay attention. She looked like she'd burst at the seams if the pressure wasn't released. "My treat. We can go to the Academy Street Café."

The café was one of my favorite places to eat in town. What the heck? I smiled my answer.

Libby giggled. "You're easy, Sarah."

"Maybe, but I'm not cheap."

❋

Over our spring salads, I asked how life as a married woman felt.

She snorted. "Not much different than before, except Cam's on the coast, and I'm here in the mountains."

"Nobody said it would be easy." I hated the trite, shallow words I said to a young woman who'd grown into one of my dearest friends.

"Truth. But I thought we'd have more time together." Libby and Cameron had married before Cam began his freshman year at Cal Poly in San Luis Obispo, a five-and-a-half-hour drive over three hundred and fifty miles away. Libby stayed here as she couldn't register for Cal Poly until next semester. She passed the time wisely by attending Cerro Coso College here in Bishop to get some of her prerequisites out of the way.

"Didn't Frank spring for a week in Hawaii?"

"Yeah, he did." Her face softened at the mention of her new father-in-law. "You know he and I didn't get along at first."

I snuffled my laugh. I remembered Frank Scherwin meeting his son Cameron and me on the outskirts of town, ordering the boy home, and telling me to keep Libby away from him. "Yes, I remember."

"But he's turned out to be the best guy in the world. I wish I could've had him for a father instead of Grant." Ugly memories shadowed behind her eyes. Her father had murdered her mother. The gleam of excitement she'd shown minutes before was stamped out.

"Maybe you had to endure life with your father so you could appreciate Frank."

She pushed her radicchio around the plate with her fork.

Irene, Academy Street Café's owner, stood at the table with our lunch orders. Libby's face changed, shifting gears from a sulky teenager to a young woman bringing good news.

Irene knew us well enough to predict our routine. We shared halves of the tuna sandwich. One of us ordered a bowl of minestrone, the other a tuna sandwich. Irene split the bowl of soup into two cups in the kitchen so we didn't mess the table up too much.

I took a bite of the sandwich. Libby's eyes widened. "Okay, do you want to know why I asked you to lunch?"

"It's because I'm a sparkling conversationalist. You haven't even asked about the new car. Rusty loves it, by the way."

An impatient wave of the hand made that irrelevant. "I have news. Big news." She sat back in her chair, eyes bright, lips pursed as if to lock in her secret lest they'd spill it before its time. "I can't wait any longer."

"Okay, shoot."

Her voice sank to a whisper. "Frank Scherwin has put in his retirement papers."

I dropped my spoon into the soup, splattering minestrone over my plate. "What? How soon?"

"I thought this might be a surprise. It's not general knowledge, but Cam said I could tell you. He thinks your boyfriend Jake might like to try for the position."

Would he? Would he even consider it? His life is in Petaluma, northern California. He's there for his career as a lieutenant at Petaluma Police. His father still lives in the area even though his half-brother, Wesley, lives here in Bishop. Would Jake even think this over? "I don't know."

"Well, you won't know if you don't tell him about it." She sat back so proud of herself that I could again see her delight. She sounded a bit like me. I guess I'd better let Jake know.

"I'll call him tonight." I sat back in my chair, my gut churning with such excitement that I lost my appetite.

# Chapter Three

After lunch, I ran home to get a box of clothing. At Layers, I hauled in the box I wanted to give to Tiffani. We were the same size and build. I had no use for the dressier clothing I used for the courts in LA. Tiffani was a bit of a clothes horse, a small-town girl with big-city aspirations. Her long blond hair made her seem misplaced from the Southern California coastal beauties. So, I brought her a few dresses from my LA professional days that I wouldn't need here. On top was a favorite deep blue velvet blazer I'd tried to wear here in my first two months. It just never felt right in Bishop. I'd just picked it up from the cleaners and left a note for Tiffani in her inbox as to where to find the clothes.

I went out front to check on the new manager, Javier. He'd been a blessing to me and the shop, especially with the café expansion. It made so much sense to have a manager who could bake as well as manage people and the books. I'd handed the ledgers over to Javier last month. He was working on entering sales, employee, and supply information into a database that would streamline activities that took me hours. It made my decision to go back to my career of court reporting so much easier. I knew Layers would be in good hands. He had everything well under control, which allowed me time to work on the Christmas Fair. He even had tasteful Christmas music playing on the overhead sound system, the volume low enough to hear but not loud enough to annoy.

After a short break outside, Rusty lumbered up the stairs with me to the office. He plopped onto his cozy office bed and watched as I moved from laptop to file cabinet and back. I spent some time on the phone, contacting merchants and crafters who were interested in hosting a table at the fair. So far, I'd lined up eleven positives and had a list of twenty-one to call. Vendors included knitted goods, homemade salsa and hot sauce, laser-cut wooden Christmas ornaments, and a booth offering replica vintage toys. It was a good start.

Then I considered the activities. I'd convinced some local nonprofits to sponsor each activity. A scavenger hunt was always fun. I planned to print out a list of hunt clues for older kids and a pictured one for the younger ones. Maybe make more than one list so that everyone isn't looking for the same thing at a particular booth. Each vendor would have a unique stamp to mark the list when a kid found a treasure. Any participant who fills up their sheet with the correct stamps gets a prize. Oh, now I had to make a list for scavenger hunt prizes—and merchants to donate.

Tom and Anna Gibson, my aunt and uncle, own a pack outfit. They bought a table with an eye to scheduling next year's rides. They had volunteered to bag up some Christmas-themed sweets and treats, brainstorming cute names like Penguin Poop for chocolate chips. Grinch Burgers for mints, Elf Bait for M&Ms,

white chocolate chips would become Snow Bunnies, and goobers would be named Reindeer Droppings. I wasn't sure which names or treats they'd choose, but it promised to be interesting.

Layers Bakery would sponsor a gingerbread man dress-up-table for kids. Gingerbread cookies were pre-baked. Each child would decorate their cookie and either eat it or take it home. Donations would be happily accepted for Layer's nonprofit, Better Off Baking, or BOB. Melody had been inspired by Libby's about-face, from a continuation school and one step away from failing, to becoming a hard-working, responsible member of a team with a high school diploma. BOB's goal was to help kids on the bad conduct fence learn adult workplace skills.

I tapped 'save' on my laptop keyboard and closed the page. I'd been at it for two hours. It was time for a break for Rusty and me. I snapped the leash on his collar, and we trotted downstairs and out the back door. The autumn temperatures had cooled to the mid-sixties with high fifties forecast for the upcoming week. Puffy cumulus clouds wafted overhead, already beginning their evening dissipation. The air smelled clean with a hint of rabbitbrush and dust. It was the desert, after all.

I followed Rusty to the parking lot. The lot bordered a perpendicular utility alley used for deliveries and refuse pick-up. Directly south of Layers was the High Sierra Coins and Collectibles shop perched on the corner of South Main and Lagoon Streets. A vacant auto repair garage sat next to the coin shop.

Rusty sniffed weeds growing at the base of the power pole at the alley entrance. Bishop was quiet midweek with little through traffic on Main Street. I clearly heard an engine running nearby. I guided Rusty to the dirt path between the Layers parking lot and the coin shop. He didn't notice the correction and snorted toward the back of the garage. I followed, listening for sounds of a car coming. I wouldn't want to get run over.

What I heard instead was two men talking. One man's voice was loud.

Norman Escher. I recognized the distinctive nasal timbre though I hadn't heard it in over a decade. "You can't do this. I didn't sign on for this." His petulant tone rose above the noise of the dark coupe parked running next to the coin shop building. Rusty sniffed the air and dismissed whatever had caught his attention. I pulled back to the Layers building, waiting for the car to pass.

Escher appeared, standing next to the old Celica I'd always seen him drive. Another man followed, a bald, hulking figure in a black tracksuit. The man shoved a gym bag filled with something bulky at Norman. He opened his arms, and catching the bag almost knocked him over. With that, the tall man wheeled around, got into the sedan, and peeled out.

I ducked back onto South Main Street with a puzzled Rusty behind me until the Celica's taillights whizzed by heading north on Main Street.

# Chapter Four

I'd planned to call Jake during Rusty's walk, but the scenario I'd just witnessed was too intriguing to interrupt. But I couldn't make any sense of it, so I boxed up both and packed them away in my mind. I'd call Jake a little later.

Walking under the tree-lined sidewalk along South Warren Street, Rusty sniffed and peed while I punched the number for Frank Scherwin.

"Sarah, what a coincidence. I was going to call you today."

"Oh yeah? How do I rate? The police chief calls me."

"Yeah, I have some news, and I want you to know before it hits the paper. The press release goes out tomorrow."

"Let me guess. You're announcing your retirement."

"Libby couldn't keep it to herself, could she?"

"She's pretty excited. She sees what a burden this position is to you and wants you to be happy."

"That kid is something, isn't she?" I heard the smile

in his response. "I can't believe my judgment was off so bad with her."

"I know what you mean. Her appearance is a challenge for us old folks to get past."

He snorted. "Yeah, that's true. But I'm glad I saw it. She's a real good addition to our family. Even my wife likes her."

"What's your retirement date?"

"The end of the year. I'll take some time off before that to burn my leave."

"Vacation plans? Or are you going to launch right into your photography business?"

"Nothing's decided yet. Probably iron out plans in the next week or so. Nancy wants to spend a couple of weeks in Maui over Christmas. We'll see."

"Well, good luck to you, Frank." I cleared my throat. "Any idea who's going to replace you?"

Frank sighed, buying time before he answered. "There's a good pool of candidates already. I don't think the city will need to launch a full-blown employment search."

"Mitch Foster?" I'd tangled with Mitch earlier this year and didn't think much of his investigative skills. His leadership abilities wouldn't be any better.

"Nah, Mitch has a lot of growing to do before he can lead a department."

"Glad to hear it."

"And are your candidates all in-house?" Within the department, there couldn't be more than one or two who had the educational qualifications to apply. I had to know.

"Aren't you the little fisherman?" He chuckled, and I saw his paunch shaking with the humor of it all. "You just can't let a mystery go unsolved."

"I'm sorry, Frank. I guess I was born nosey." I waited while Frank collected himself. I hadn't been born nosey. My curiosity had taken hold the minute I set foot back in Bishop. My cousin had been murdered under my nose, and the local law enforcement had taken the easy way to solve her murder. I'd known there was more—much more. In the following weeks, I'd made a nuisance of myself but managed to put the cops onto the correct trail. The murderer was found. During the following months, partly because I was local—born and raised in Bishop—and partly because I got results, people began to trust me with their secrets. "So, answer the question. Please."

He laughed again. "No, the city is looking outside Bishop, but staying in California."

It was my turn to laugh. "Okay. I guess I've gotten all I'm going to from you today."

"Libby will get in touch with you about the retirement party. She's organizing it."

"Okay, Frank. I won't say goodbye. I know I'll see you around."

"Yep, we're staying in Bishop. Nancy and I love it here."

"What's not to love?"

# Chapter Five

"Sarah." Back in the office at Layers, Jake's deep voice over the phone tickled a place in my heart and made me smile.

"Hey, you. I've got some news. I'm not sure you're interested in his job, but Frank Scherwin from Bishop PD is retiring at the end of the year."

"No kidding." He laughed. "We took bets on how long it would take for you to call me."

"You and Frank? I didn't know you knew him."

"We've talked a few times over the past months."

"Oh, since Reginald's murder?"

"Yeah, sometime around then."

Why was he being so evasive? Irritation squirmed through me. "Okay, I just thought you might be interested in applying. I know we haven't talked about our distant future, but getting this job could bring you and me a lot closer."

"Yes, it would. I've got some business up here to consider too." From the tone of his voice, I could tell that someone walked in. He must be at the office. "Listen, I've got to go. I'll be down this weekend on Saturday. We'll talk then."

Jake was putting me off. There was no getting around it. Maybe he didn't want to get married, have kids. But he was right about one thing. We hadn't talked about where we would live. I know he loved Petaluma and his father lived nearby in another small town, Novato. But I had family here in Bishop. I'd left once before and wasn't going to make that mistake again. I hadn't been miserable in Los Angeles, but when I got home here in the high desert, I realized I had been like a sagging Mylar balloon, floating from one place to another. I needed Bishop to be my home base.

What if Jake decided to stay in Petaluma? What would I do then? Lord, I didn't have the answer.

Sitting at my desk, I quashed my disappointment and decided to focus on what I could manage. That would be the Christmas Fair.

Paula from the chamber of commerce had secured the venue. Charles Brown Auditorium at the TriCounty Fairgrounds in Bishop would host our event. As far as I was concerned, Paula had done the heavy lifting. All I had to do was round up some enthusiastic vendors and volunteers to help set up. Bishop was great for that. Christmas was always a wonderful holiday, as well as a family-oriented community. The Christmas Parade and Tree Lighting in City Park would be at the beginning of December. By then, sugar plum fairies would be dancing in youngsters' heads, making the fair a fun place to finish shopping, enjoy a game or two, and join in some fun.

The Bishop Lions Club had volunteered to take on the "Decorate the Tree" booth. The Lions would trim the tree with garlands and lights, then position it to the right of the stage. Three other nonprofits have committed to sponsoring ornament decorating booths. One of the groups was the Bishop Education Foundation. This year's head was a woman who made comedian Will Farrell look brilliant. I'd put off calling her until now. I was already disappointed over my conversation with Jake, so talking to Wilma wouldn't sink me any lower.

She started right in. "You want the Ed Foundation to sponsor a table or man it?" I stood, pacing from the window to the door. Rusty lifted his head, watched me for a minute, then went back to sleep.

I glanced at the wall clock. Javier would've closed the shop by now. Yes, I heard a reciprocating saw, noise from the electrician installing the lights in the café. I was getting a headache.

"Staffing is crucial, Wilma. You'll need supplies, like glue, glitter, scissors…" I had to talk over her to finish. "Safety scissors, of course, Wilma. Whatever it takes to make an ornament. The premise is simple. Your audience is young children. You charge a dollar per ornament or whatever is appropriate. If there are a half dozen or more prototypes of ornaments that they can copy, it will be easier for them. Then they can take their treasure and decorate the tree nearby or take the ornament home."

"Where are we going to get the money for that? That stuff's expensive…" Wilma went on, gnawing at my ear. A few moments later, I stood at the window, looking out, wishing I was anywhere but on the phone with her. In the alley below, the blue Celica cruised to a stop. Norman unfolded himself from behind the steering wheel, marched around, and opened the sliding aluminum door to the vacant garage next to his business.

He drove the Celica inside and closed the door behind him.

Something wasn't right. Besides Wilma.

I shook my head, wondering at the mysterious actions of my neighbor Norman Escher. What was he up to?

# Chapter Six

The next morning, Anna stood in the Layers office, shifting from one foot to the other. With her short, brown, cropped hair and tanned, oval face, she represented how I thought of the ideal outdoor Owens Valley woman. Her red Layers Bakery polo shirt was tucked neatly into her chinos. Capable and compassionate, she loved her family more than anything. She was my mother's sister-in-law, and they'd always been more like sisters. She was a second mother to me. In fact, with her children, Mark and Melody, we used to call our mothers 'the moms.' They were a unit, cohesive teachers of courtesies and moral conduct. Melody and I paid attention better than Mark did.

"I'm sorry, Sarah, but I just heard from the orthopedic surgeon's office. They've scheduled Mark's surgery for tomorrow. I'll need the rest of this week off and next, maybe even more. In fact, I may not come back." She stared down at me as I sat at the desk.

"I'm surprised you stayed this long, Anna. You've always got something to do at home."

She frowned. "Always. But this is different. My son needs me."

"Of course." I smiled, mildly surprised that she was so uncomfortable with this request. "Mom said surgery was possible, so I penciled out next week's schedule without you. I planned for one week, but we can easily work in your time off for another five days. Unless you want to make this permanent?"

"Um. Yes, I do. I don't know how long it will take Mark to recover, and I want to be there for him. It's unfair to keep you hanging."

I smiled. "It's no problem, Anna. We'll find someone to replace you. You're doing the right thing. We'll start looking for someone immediately." This would mean more hours for me until we found Anna's replacement. I didn't want to leave the burden of hiring to Javier, although it seemed like a good time to let him learn.

Her face melted with relief. "Thanks. We'll consider this my notice, then." She stood for a second, and I thought she might have more to say. "This place is... was Melody's dream. I'm so happy that you've made my daughter's plans come to fruition." With a grin, she added, "With Better Off Baking, it's even better than she planned."

She had touched a precious place in my heart. As an only child, my cousin Melody was more of a sister to me. It meant everything to bring this idea to life. "I'm glad you feel that way. It's set up so that this will continue after I go back to work. Wesley even approves." Melody's husband, Wesley, had inherited the bakery upon his wife's death, although he didn't have a clue how to operate it. Melody had hired me to manage the burgeoning bakery business before she died so suddenly. The idea was for her to build the Better Off Baking nonprofit for kids at risk. While that didn't happen, it was a no-brainer to put my own plans on hold until we found a manager to take over. I would continue working on the Better Off Baking program.

Anna dropped to the chair opposite me. "So, it's for sure? You're going to work for the court?"

"I am, yes." I thought of all that had gone on in the past six months since I'd moved home. The major challenge was putting off my career as a court reporter to manage Layers Bakery. "I love the bakery, but I'm looking forward to going back to what I know." I'd be resuming the career I'd begun in Los Angeles. The county retirement I'd earned would be combined with the Inyo County Courts' when my career was over. My job would be different in the added chores, and the salary wasn't as much as I'd had, but the cost of living in Bishop wasn't as high. I'd have an income sufficient to allow me to rent my own apartment or house. I was looking forward to the future.

"By the way, Tiffani looks fabulous in the blue blazer you gave her." My phone chimed an incoming text. Anna stood. "I'd better get back to the counter."

It was Jake. *I'll be there Saturday midday.* I expected he'd do what had become routine. He'd stop by my parents' house, where I lived for now. Then he'd head to Wilkerson, south of town, to the small enclave where Wesley lived. He'd stay there with his brother.

My stomach tightened with the notion of the conversation to come. I loved Jake and believed that he loved me. With marriage a distant inevitability, the conclusion of where we would live together after we married was the question. Petaluma or Bishop? In Petaluma, Jake was on an upward career path and, given time, might achieve his goal of being the police chief. Then, too, his elderly father required Jake's attention. And Jake had his friends that he'd known all his life, as well as his colleagues. I chewed my lip as I considered how a move across the state would impact Jake.

But I was more confirmed than ever to stay on this side of the Sierras. I'd missed my family and the friends I'd grown up with. They were all people who had my back, like Mom and Dad, Tom and Anna, Wesley, Emily, and Matt Kilbride.

Jake and I would talk about it, but I surely couldn't see any way to meet in the middle.

# Chapter Seven

Rusty and I went for a spin up South Warren Street. The warm breeze smelled of the desert sage as it rustled the few elm leaves left on the trees. I savored being home while I tried to work solutions for Jake's and my problem. I should just wait until we talk face to face on Saturday. It was possible something had changed in his life. I felt more than selfish being so obstinate about staying in Bishop. I didn't know how I could compromise.

When I got back, Libby was drying her hands. The kitchen was immaculate. Counters and worktables were clear and wiped down. All food was secured and put away in the assigned shelf or refrigerator. I checked on Javier and got some good news. "I hired my sister-in-law to cover for Anna while she's off. That okay?"

I nodded, grateful he'd found such a quick solution. "She's decided she won't be back. If Rosalyn works out, you might consider asking her to stay on permanently. Do you remember where the employment paperwork is in the desk?"

"Already done." He gave me a thumbs-up and plated an *au pain chocolate* for a customer.

When I walked into the kitchen, Libby sat on her stool at the empty worktable, her phone face down. Her eyes widened with an expectant look as I unhooked Rusty's leash and shooed him upstairs. I said, "You look like you need a friend."

She chuckled. "You were chewing your lip. That means *you* need to talk." We looked at each other, speculating on the state of our minds. The thought struck us at the same moment.

We hooted at each other. "Look at you, turning into a Sensible Libby." I put my arm around her shoulders and gave them a squeeze. Then I sat next to her. "What's bugging you, friend?"

"You." She turned to face me. "You look miserable. I know things are going good here, and the fair is moving along, so I assume it must be Jake."

I sighed. As much as I'd like to think I could conceal my miseries from friends and family, there were those who could read me well enough. Libby was one of those from whom I couldn't hide anything. "You're pretty smart for a teenager."

A grin spread across her face. "College of hard knocks, like my granddad used to say."

"Not for you, my dear. You're going to a university after this semester at Cerro Coso."

"Yeah. Right." She gave a lavish eye roll. "But I'd like to talk about you. Are you having trouble with the distance between you?"

"Sure. Aren't you?"

She nodded. "The simplest issues are complicated by the fact that we're separated by miles and hours of driving."

I nodded. "Sometimes texting, Facetime, and phone calls don't do the trick."

"Yeah, they can make a simple conversation way more difficult. Last week Cam said he was trying to psych out my feelings about us having Christmas with his family. We got into it over what he thought I meant instead of what I said."

"We haven't gotten that far yet. We're still trying to figure out where we will live. We haven't talked about marriage or anything that serious."

Libby didn't say anything.

"I don't want to leave Bishop, and he doesn't want to leave Petaluma. Can we continue a relationship with this distance between us? I don't know."

Libby was silent.

"What I do know is that I feel incredibly selfish for not budging on a move."

"You have to take care of yourself." Her tiny hand grasped mine. It felt warm and strong. "One of the things Frank taught me is that if a police officer goes running into a hot situation and gets hurt or killed, he cannot help anyone else."

"The application might be a bit different here, but I get what you're saying. I'm no good to anyone if I'm falling apart. I'm not going to be saving the world, but I do need to stand up for myself."

"Now you got it." One quick, sharp nod. "The other part of that equation is that you shouldn't give up. Talk things out."

Libby was right. We weren't the only ones to carry on a love affair over long distance. Libby and Cam had obviously found solutions to a few of their issues. Jake and I could too.

# Chapter Eight

The next morning, Javier and I were in the office. He was patiently explaining the new payroll and accounting software in which he was interested. I planned on learning the program so I could help if needed.

My phone rang. The caller ID read *Harlan Evers*. What could he want? Although we'd had a dust-up months ago, through Libby, we'd managed a respectful truce. Truce or not, it was a surprise to see his name on my phone.

"Harlan?"

"Yes, Sarah. It's me."

"What can I do for you?"

"Well, it's kind of a delicate situation. I'd rather not discuss it over the phone. Can you meet me at school?"

"I don't know. Am I in trouble?"

Evers chuckled. "Not this time. That curiosity of yours is just what I may need."

Intrigued, I replied. "I can be there in ten minutes. Will that work?"

"Yes, yes." He spoke to someone in the background. "Yes, that'll be great. See you soon."

The guidance office was in the same place as it had been in September. On the ground floor of the main building, the door was closed with a *come back later* sign hanging from a clip on the door window.

I knocked on the door, and Harlan Evers opened it. A youngish man, he appeared to be in his late twenties. We stood at eye level, and while I was tall for a woman, he came in at average height for a man. He'd styled his short, cropped, brown hair with every hair in place. His thin-lipped smile reached vivid blue eyes that shone with intelligence. A pale blue oxford shirt, khakis, and dark brown leather loafers completed the look of a serious high school guidance counselor.

Nothing had changed in the office. His cubicle was the largest and at a window. Books and binders organized on shelves and papers on his desk sat all in squared, tidy formation.

"Sarah, thanks for coming."

"Of course. You made it sound intriguing."

He cocked his head to one side. "It could be serious, but it's too early to tell yet." He waved a hand at a vacant chair across from his desk.

As I sat, my curiosity was piqued. "Why don't you tell me what's going on."

"Let me introduce you to the guy in the know." Over the cubicle, he motioned behind me. I heard rustling, then a man of the same age entered. "This is Sam Gallagher." He introduced me to the man, and Harlan stepped aside.

Gallagher sat in Harlan's seat and met my gaze across the desk. He could've been Harlan's twin. They were even dressed the same, but in different colored shirts. Harlan continued the introduction. "Sam is a sixth-grade teacher at Bishop Elementary School. He has a student named Madison Hall. I'll let him tell you the rest."

After a reassuring nod from Harlan, Gallagher began his story. "This is a difficult situation. Madison seems to be missing. That in itself is a big problem. But there's more. Her parents are in Reno, and she's been in the care of her grandfather."

"What is the problem?" Wondering what comprised the *so much more* to this story, I mentally gave in. I was already hooked.

"When Maddie didn't show up at school, the school called first and was told she was sick. I thought I'd offer to bring her schoolwork by so she didn't fall behind. I called the phone number the front office was given for the grandfather. The person answered, 'High Desert Coins.' Then I told him who I was and that I was calling to see if I could come by to drop off Maddie's assignments and books. He said no, that she wasn't feeling well and was with him, resting."

"That's all he said?"

"Yes. But I don't believe him. He acted nervous, which made me worry even more about Maddie. She's a great kid, bright and outspoken. She doesn't have a filter most days."

I pondered this information. "Do you feel that not having a filter puts her at risk?"

He tipped his head as he considered his answer. "She can anger people. She calls them like she sees them, and not everyone is okay with her unvarnished perception of the truth."

"Have you ever seen how her grandfather interacts with her?"

He bowed his head, inspecting his fingernails. "Not firsthand, but one of the aides came to me last week. She told me the grandfather yelled at Maddie in the parking lot so loud and long, that she considered calling the police. Now I wish she had."

"What you're not saying to me is that you're concerned about her welfare, right?"

He nodded.

"Why don't you call the police? They can do a welfare check on her to see if she's okay."

"Before the call ended this morning, Escher, that's his name..."

"Wait. What's his name?" The hair on my forearms prickled.

"Escher, Norman Escher. Anyway, he told me not to call the police. He said she wasn't truant or anything. That she was merely feeling under the weather and there was no need to involve the authorities."

I'll bet he did. There was something going on here. Three separate incidents with Norman Escher in two days. I hadn't been sure I would look for Madison until now. But the police have many more resources. This wasn't enough to call and report her missing. Maybe teacher reporting was the route to take. I scrounged around my brain to recall state law about crime reporting for teachers. "As school personnel, you are obligated to report neglect or abuse."

"Right. But this falls into a gray area. We don't know if she's being abused. I've never seen any outward marks nor behavioral clues for either neglect or abuse."

Harlan spoke. "We're afraid if we call wolf too many

times, we won't be taken seriously when it's really needed."

I didn't need to tell them what I'd seen over the past two days. Even that wouldn't be enough to report her missing to the cops. "Okay. I understand your perspective. I'm not sure you're right, but I get it." I shifted to include Harlan in my gaze. "Why tell me?"

Harlan sighed as he perched on the corner of his desk. "You have a bit of a reputation. Through your questions, you've led police to two murderers."

At my protest, Harlan's voice grew stronger. "You can't deny that you're a curious lady. Why, even if we don't ask you, I'd bet that you would go out searching for Maddie, given what you know."

I certainly was gaining a reputation in my hometown. "What'd you mean, if you hadn't asked me? Didn't you just do that?"

*Chapter Nine*

Harlan texted and then copied a picture of Madison Hall that Sam had brought so that I had a print copy and one on my phone. I had questions, most of which Sam answered. He gave me a general idea of where Maddie shopped and hung out when not at school or home, addresses of her best friends, where her grandfather lived, and her parents' address.

Back at Layers, I told Javier and Libby that I would be working on fair business. I picked up Rusty and loaded him in my brand-new-to-me Subaru SUV. I was sure to use the remote liftgate. First stop was Maddie's home address. She lived on Short Street. The street was two blocks long, a short street, indeed. The mid-forties one-story house looked locked up tight. A hip-high chain link fence surrounded the property, including a gate with wheels across the driveway. From its placement on the block, I was fairly certain there wasn't an alley with access to the rear of the house. In Bishop, alleys were common and used often. I looked around and saw no neighbors outside.

I swung my leg over the gate and walked through the *porte cochere*. The backyard was enormous, the lawn and trees still green with summer growth. I walked the back and side perimeters of the house slowly, noting locked doors and windows. No Christmas decorations. Yes, the Hall family was out of town.

Retracing my steps, I got back into my car. Starting it up, I drove around the corner in case one of the neighbors saw me. I pressed the button for park and let the car idle while my thumping heart calmed. What next?

After five minutes, I decided my heart couldn't take too much sleuthing in one day. I'd brought my list of merchants to contact, so I changed my focus to the Christmas Fair.

Sierra Wave Vintage Clothing Store on the corner of West Pine and North Warren Streets was on my 'interested' list. The smell of worn leather, cinnamon-spiked pinecones, and pine-scented candles met me as I entered. Holly garlands trimmed the beam over the cash register. Soft carols played a welcoming tune. A young woman with sun-bleached shoulder-length hair, full cheeks, and an enthusiastic smile met me.

"Mmm, it smells wonderful in here. Are you the owner, Victoria Turley?"

"I am."

"I'm Sarah Murray from the Christmas Fair. We've spoken on the phone."

"Oh yes. I've been expecting you."

"Did you have something in mind for the fair? We have several different choices for vendors. You can donate a prize or sponsor a table for crafts. There're also a number of fun events that you can sponsor or volunteer to help."

"I'd like to rent a table and sell our merchandise. We

have quite a selection of Christmas ornaments and such that I'd like to offer. We'll make the prices cheap enough for families to afford."

I took out my tablet. "We have four spaces left."

While I pulled up the floor plan, Victoria rolled her eyes. "Wow, I thought I was getting in early enough to have a good spot. What do you have left?"

"This one near the front door might be good for you."

She eyed it critically. "Yes, that'll do. It will be cold when the door opens, though."

"Nobody will think it unusual if you're wearing a jacket, scarf, and mittens, will they?"

She giggled at the idea.

Before I put the tablet away, I switched to a page with Maddie's picture. "On another note... Have you ever seen this girl before? I was told she shops here."

The picture rotated so Victoria could see it. "Oh yes, Maddie. She's a regular. I see her mom and her in here often." With a proud smile, she said, "Our stock rotates pretty fast."

"Have you seen her yesterday or today?"

"Yeah. Just yesterday, without her mom. I said she should've been in school, but she said she had a pass. She didn't seem so happy without her mother." Victoria shrugged at the memory. "I hope she's not in trouble."

"Not that I know of." I had a thought. "When she left, did she walk, use a bike or..."

She squinted, remembering yesterday. "Oh, a big black sedan showed up at the curb. She didn't notice it at first. When she left the shop, I thought the driver hailed her and she got in. The car drove away."

"What kind of car was it?"

She put an index finger on her chin like it would help her recall. "A Dodge Challenger, maybe a two-door. No.

A Mustang, maybe?" She shrugged. "Camaro? Anyway, one of those muscle cars."

"Did you see the driver?"

"Uh, no. I was standing right here, and the car was parked at a bad angle." From near her vantage point, I glanced outside and noticed the slope was significant from the road's center crown. The roof would've blocked the view of the driver. Unlucky for us.

I thanked her, and as I left, she said, "I hope she's not in trouble. I thought it was her grandfather who picked her up. I assumed he bought a new car. Maddie said something about him coming into some money."

I considered the most diplomatic response. "I hope she's not in trouble too." As I walked out the door, I chewed my lip, worried that she was, indeed, in trouble.

# Chapter Ten

Rusty and I spent the rest of the cool afternoon discretely contacting school friends, checking the bowling alley and library. Rusty especially loved the stroll we took through City Park. Just before five o'clock, we headed back to the car through the park. It would cool off tonight. I wished I had my sweater.

My phone chimed Luke Combs' song, "Better Together"—Jake's ring. I steered Rusty toward a picnic bench in the shade as I touched the icon to accept the call.

"Hey, you. What're you doing today?"

"Working on the Christmas Fair, mostly. I've been talking to merchants about doing different things for the fair."

"Sounds boring." He was at work. In the background, a series of tones chimed, then a dispatcher's monotoned voice, although the words were vague.

"It's not. I love meeting new people and seeing folks I haven't seen in years."

"You're more of a people person than I am."

I chuckled. "You say that, but everyone"—I remembered Mark—"okay, almost everyone you meet thinks the world of you."

"Hmm, Mark."

I chuckled. "Being able to get along with most people is a requirement for a police chief, isn't it?"

"Yes." He had a strange tone in his voice. I couldn't make out what he might mean.

"And you have to be a politician, right?"

"Yes," he answered flatly. "That's the opposite of what a street cop wants to be."

"Maybe. You could be right. Some parts of our job get easier if you know how to talk to people."

"What's going on? You sound different, like something's bothering you."

He gave an exasperated sigh. "Sarah, I've got a dozen things eating at me. I'm distracted and not focused on this conversation. I shouldn't have called now. I'm sorry."

"Jake, there's nothing to be sorry about. You have a demanding job and get pulled every which way all the time."

His voice softened. "Thanks for understanding, Sarah, sweetheart. I'm lucky to have you."

"Me too. Why don't you call tomorrow before work?" After work would be too late. He worked the swing shift and was scheduled to get off work at two o'clock in the morning. I wasn't very conversational at that hour.

"I'll do that. I love you. Remember that."

His words chilled me. As I disconnected, I wondered what he meant when he said, 'remember that.' Was he preparing me for bad news? Had I said or done something that bothered him? I wanted to call Wesley to talk over this phone call with Jake's brother, but that sounded too junior high.

Speaking of junior high, I worried about Maddie Hall. Now a sixth grader, I mentally crossed my fingers she'd make it to junior high school. Where was she? Was she safe with her grandfather? I needed to find a home address for him. Sam said the only address they had for Norman was a PO Box. That wasn't any help.

In the end, Rusty and I went for a walk. Where East Line Street meets the city limits, a graded dirt path followed the canal. A great deal of Owens Valley water flowed south to Los Angeles under the ownership of the Los Angeles Department of Water and Power. Locals called it DWP.

A short walk along the canal made me feel better. Rusty found a stick he liked better than his tennis ball, so we walked while I practiced my stick pitching until it was time to go home.

## Chapter Eleven

I tossed and turned all night worrying about Maddie Hall. Wondering if she was tied up and hidden away in some anonymous room where no one will find her. Nightmares of her being assaulted, beaten, or worse kept me awake.

As I lay in bed staring into the darkness pondering all these uncertainties, a plan began to emerge. Tomorrow morning, first thing, I'd text Harlan to see if Maddie made it to school. School started at eight-ten. The inquiry would have to wait until after roll call, about eight-thirty. Then, secondly, I'd try to contact Norman. He kept erratic hours at the store. In truth, more than once, I'd wondered how he made a living. I rarely saw customers. Since I'd be at Layers early, I'd walk over and knock on the door. He might answer even if he wasn't open. If he saw me, he'd know who it was. We'd waved to each other while coming and going, but we never really spoke. I had no idea if he'd open the door.

The idea was to ask him straight up—where is Maddie? There was no advantage in being coy. How I proceeded from there depended on his answer. I'd tell him what I'd learned about Maddie being picked up by the black Challenger. He might know who owns it. Maybe he sent someone to pick up his granddaughter. The question of why remained.

At eight-thirty, I texted Harlan, asking if Maddie was at school. After a few minutes, he said Sam told him no. On to the next item.

After a talk with Norman, I hope I'd know more about Maddie's situation. Part three of my plan was to call Kelly for a cup of coffee at Layers Café. I'd talk to him about the missing person status of Maddie Hall.

The bright sun startled me as I emerged from the Layers kitchen. I slipped on my sunglasses and walked across the alley. The clock in the kitchen read eight thirty-five. I didn't expect him to be open, but I wanted to check the hours on the front door sign. I'd try a peek through the shades and see if he was inside.

With the shades closed up tight, there was no chance to see into the store. The door sign read *11:00 a.m. to 4:00 p.m.* I made a mental note to return at eleven o'clock.

An urgency was beginning to seep into me. I worried about what could've happened to the young girl. I crossed my fingers that she was in Reno or Palmdale shopping with girlfriends, but it didn't seem realistic.

I decided not to wait to contact Kelly until after a conversation with Norman. Kelly had rotated schedules and was now working day shift, 7:00 a.m. until 3:00 p.m. I texted him asking for a coffee break at Layers whenever he was free. His answer was immediate. He was on his way, *TT from S Bis.* I'd quickly learned Kelly's law enforcement shorthand. This meant *travel time from south Bishop.*

In ten minutes, we were seated in Layers' cozy café, stirring our respective coffees. Tiffani, our unpredictable barista, had whipped up a nice pumpkin spice latte for Kelly and a chai for me. The café was growing into a comfortable place to ruminate over a hot or cold coffee in the morning. Bookshelves lined one wall, and banquette seating had been constructed in both front windows. Tonight, after we closed, the electrician would complete the lighting. Tomorrow the painters would do the finish work. The hope was to encourage lounging. A half dozen tables and chairs filled the space from the door to where the queue poles began for counter service. Today, several moms drifted in after dropping kids off at school. A pair sat in one banquette seat, and three others chose a table on the opposite side of the room.

All kept their distance from the giant deputy in the middle of the room. I smiled at the vibe I felt when the women came in. Because of Kelly's presence, they felt safer. I know I certainly felt that. Kelly and I had been friends in high school and drifted apart when I got married and moved away. It wasn't too long after my divorce from Blaine and return to Bishop that I bumped into Kelly. We picked up our friendship where we'd left off. He'd saved my life once in the recent past and helped me find Cousin Melody's murderer. What all this leads up to is that I trust Kelly. With my life.

Kelly got right to the point. "Is this a social call, or do you have something on your mind?"

I grinned. "While I love visiting with you, there's something I'd like to discuss with you."

Kelly's lips thinned with amusement. "Shoot."

I stirred the cream into my chai. "I don't know what the laws are around reporting a missing juvenile."

"Not everything is a mystery, Sarah." An impatient

scowl crossed his face. "You just tell me what's bothering you, and I'll figure out the law stuff."

"All right." I pushed ahead with relief that something might be done to find Maddie. "A teacher acquaintance has come to me reporting one of his students has missed several days of school. When the attendance office called home, they got an answering machine. Then they called an emergency contact person, her grandfather. He told the school that her parents were out of town, and she was staying with him. She'd felt under the weather, and he kept her home."

"That doesn't sound unreasonable." Kelly's gaze searched my face, knowing me well enough that there was more information to come.

"Right. So, this teacher can't report the kid as missing because the explanation does sound so acceptable." I paused, rounding up the words I'd corralled earlier when I planned this conversation. "The thing is that the teacher doesn't believe the excuse. He called the grandfather on the premise that he could bring homework home for the girl so she wouldn't fall behind. The grandfather said no. He about flipped out at my friend and told him not to come to his house. As an aside, the school only has a PO Box address for the grandfather, no physical address."

Kelly's eyes narrowed. "I see where you're going with this. You want me to search for this kid. But unofficially, without a missing person report."

"There's more." I told him what Sam had relayed to me about Norman shouting at Maddie at school. Then, I told him about my own observations in the past few days. That I'd overheard an argument with the guy in the Challenger in the alley between our shops, and Norman had bought an expensive car, without apparent means.

And last, what the vintage shop owner had told me about Maddie being picked up in a black muscle car, could be a Mustang or Challenger.

"Are we talking about two different cars here? A Challenger or a Mustang?"

"The shop owner wasn't sure. She couldn't tell the model from where she stood, so she couldn't say. There could be two cars."

"Hmm. Did it sound like the girl was reluctant to get in the car?"

I shook my head. "I didn't ask. I didn't want to alarm anyone over her disappearance."

"Hmm. The shop lady would've mentioned if there'd been any resistance on the girl's part."

"I think so too."

"What's the girl's name?" I gave him what information I had, including the vintage shop owner's address and name. "And the grandfather?"

"Norman Escher."

"Owner of the coin shop next door?"

I nodded.

"He's a piece of work. There have been rumors for years that he fenced stolen goods."

"Bad luck for him that there isn't much in the way of crime in Bishop."

"Could be why he doesn't have two nickels to rub together."

I wondered to what lengths he'd go to put extra cash in his wallet.

"That black Mustang is a noticeable vehicle here in Bishop." He was right. Most cars were SUVs for families and pickup trucks for ranch work. "I'll keep an eye out."

# Chapter Twelve

K elly drained his coffee mug and pushed it to the center of the table. "Will Jake be coming down soon?"

"Saturday, midday."

"Edward three, Sheriff's one." Over Kelly's shoulder mic, the male dispatcher's voice cut through our conversation.

Kelly answered.

"We have an 11-54 unoccupied on Mumy Lane, west Bishop. Vehicle is a late model black Dodge two-door; parked near West Line for over a day."

Kelly mumbled into the mic. "Copy. Enroute." He stood, and every eye in the place watched him as he left.

Fifteen minutes later, Kelly was on the phone. "Can you come out here?"

"Mumy Lane? Sure. Why?"

"You'll see when you get here." He disconnected.

It wasn't like Kelly to be mysterious. I grabbed Rusty and my purse. The bakery crew was used to my coming and going. Javier was off today, but the place ran well enough without me for a few hours. That's one of the reasons I accepted when the chamber asked me to head up the Christmas Fair.

❀

Ten minutes later found me parking behind Kelly's patrol car. The black Challenger coupe sat on the shoulder at an angle almost perpendicular to Mumy Lane. Kelly's attention was riveted on the car.

He spoke to me over his shoulder. "C'mon up but don't touch anything."

Alarmed at the direction, I walked slowly, my gaze scanning my surroundings. "You got me creeped out, Kel."

"Yeah, me too."

It's a bit scary when a big, tough sheriff's deputy tells you he's creeped out.

"Is this the car?"

I scrutinized what I could from the rear. Then I moved to the side, which would be the angle at which I'd first seen the Challenger. "It sure looks like it."

"Can you describe the driver?"

"Tall, bulky, like muscle turned to fat, a bit of a belly. He was wearing a black warm-up suit."

"Hair color?"

"Oh, he was bald."

"That would be noticeable." A tiny smile tipped the corner of Kelly's generous lips. I should've remembered and told him that.

"The plate's registered to a corporation out of Lancaster, Anchorman Holdings. I don't have any more information on the owner." He pulled out latex gloves from his back pocket and a small flashlight. "Based on what you've told me, I'm calling this suspicious." He snapped the last glove on and reached for the driver-side door handle. "You stand back."

I thought he was being a bit of a drama queen. What could happen? A jack-in-the-box could pop out? But I walked back to my car anyway and leaned against the hood.

"Gun!" Kelly's voice cut through the desert. I knew this was a cop's way of warning others that a gun has been seen. But there were no other cops around. Kelly's adrenaline just shot through the roof.

Kelly straightened and spoke into his shoulder mic. Continuous radio traffic ensued, mostly without Kelly. He held his position at the driver's door but used his pen to move the pistol from under the seat. His voice rose to a yell. "A Sig P226 semi-auto. Some serious shooting power. Loaded. You stay right there, Sarah."

I opened the liftgate, and Rusty hopped out. I attached the leash because I suspected this was going to look like a circus in a minute. I didn't want Rusty loose and getting in the way. We strolled along the roadside away from the Challenger as Rusty fertilized the weeds.

A siren whooped in the distance, and I figured Kelly had asked for help. Within a minute, a white Bishop PD unit arrived parking at an angle next to Kelly's patrol car. A female patrol officer, short, stocky, with a blond ponytail, approached the black coupe. She gloved up and took the Sig from Kelly. She opened the slide, caught the round that popped out then dropped the magazine into her other hand.

An unmarked Ford sedan rolled up and pulled to a smooth stop. Quentin Powers, the sheriff's detective whom I'd met several months ago, eased out from behind the wheel. His glance took in everything. He gave a nod to me, then walked toward Kelly. The PD officer had the gun in an evidence bag with the ammunition in a separate envelope. She handed them both to the detective and went back to her unit.

Kelly explained the situation to Powers, occasionally motioning to me. I stayed where I was with an unusually patient Rusty sitting quietly beside me. When Quentin Powers caught my eye and started walking in my direction, I put Rusty away. He was fine inside the car with the windows down.

With a polite nod, Quentin Powers asked if he could talk to me.

"Of course."

I stayed where I was, leaning on the hood of my car, and Powers asked me to tell my story. I repeated what I'd told Kelly without using the names of the teachers who'd asked me to check into Maddie's disappearance. I knew he'd ask, but I didn't want to volunteer them unless they were really needed.

Finally, he asked the identities of the two teachers I'd talked to. I gave him the information making a mental note to text Harlan a warning as soon as possible.

I couldn't hold back my questions. "Quentin, why all this over a gun? I know it was concealed, but really... this seems a bit like overkill."

Powers scrutinized my face for a second, then glanced away at the Challenger. "Well, the gun was a big deal. The serial number has been etched off, so someone wants it to be untraceable." He cleared his throat and focused on the scene before us. "The really big deal is finding blood on the dashboard."

Blood? Oh, Lord. Maddie had sat there yesterday.

*Chapter Thirteen*

The idea that Maddie sat in the passenger seat of that big black Challenger stuck with me the rest of the day. I was released from the scene shortly after my interview with Quentin Powers. I couldn't shake the idea of Maddie being injured—or worse.

The time on my car's infotainment display read two o'clock. I drove back to Layers and, after another short break, stashed Rusty in his upstairs office bed. I dropped my purse, shoved my phone in my pants pocket, and walked over to the coin shop.

I realized I could be jeopardizing any case the Inyo County sheriff might build, but because it was now over two and a half days since Maddie's disappearance, I felt time was critical.

The High Sierra Coins and Collectibles seemed a bit pretentious for such a humble building. It had the distinction of being the only business in town with bars on the windows and a steel security door at the main entrance. A one-story structure with a flat roof, the stucco siding was cracked and faded. Two windows on each side of the steel security front door gave it the feel of a characterless structure built strictly for function. Mini blinds and roller shades protected the inventory from prying eyes. Even though the sign hanging in the front window said it should be open, it wasn't.

My knuckle tapped out a solid knock. The blinds in the far window parted slightly. I couldn't see who it was, but I knocked harder using all my knuckles. A minute passed before I heard the three locks on the front door unbolt. It opened wide enough to see an eyeball and some curly salt-and-pepper hair. Escher.

"Norman, it's Sarah Murray from Layers Bakery next door. I need to talk to you."

"So, talk."

"Is Maddie in there? I need to know where your granddaughter is."

"You're kidding, right?"

"No, I'm very serious." I decided to keep the police out of it.

He licked his lips. "Butt out, girlie."

"She's missed school for the last three days. She doesn't have any homework to keep her up in class."

He stepped backward, starting to close the door. I stuck my toe between the door and the jamb. "Wait. Is there something wrong? Is she too sick to do homework?"

"Get out of here. You're trespassing." He kicked my toe out of the door and slammed it.

My toe throbbing, I walked back to Layers thinking that even getting nowhere was something. Norman Escher was hiding something or someone. He was lying about Maddie being sick. If she'd been there, it would've been a simple matter of her showing her face to get me out of the front door.

I sat at my desk and rubbed my eyes, thinking over what Escher's denial could mean for Maddie. Why was she missing? Had she run away? Had her grandfather hidden her? Why? Where were her parents in all this? The possibilities were many.

Getting nowhere, I pulled out my phone and glanced at the calls.

Jake had called and left a message when I was out on Mumy Lane with Kelly. Oh no. I hope he didn't think I was avoiding him. I texted, *Sorry I missed your call. I got busy. Can you call on your lunch break?* He usually ate at nine-thirty or ten o'clock. I'd be awake then.

*Can't. Will call tomorrow.* Was he upset with me? Now I'd have to tell him about my involvement in a missing kid's case.

This day just couldn't get any worse.

# Chapter Fourteen

My observation that my day couldn't get worse was wrong.

Rusty and I had strolled down the canal and back, Mumy Lane having lost some of its appeal. I walked slowly, thinking over what had happened in the past few days. Rusty was feeling the briskness of the early December breeze. He romped and jumped, then fetched the short stick he'd selected from among the surrounding sagebrush. Eager for dinner, he loaded into the back of the Subaru with no complaints. The stick came too.

On the way home, my phone rang. *Jake.*

I answered with a cheery, "Hi, honey."

"Hey, you." His voice was soft. The police radio squawked in the background.

"You're calling from work."

"I'm in my car." He sounded tired or down. "I called because I didn't like how we left it yesterday."

"Me too."

"There's so much we don't say because we aren't

close together. I can't see your face when I tell you I love you."

"It sounds like you're feeling the same way I am." I sighed. "This distance thing is a pain."

"Well, just hearing your voice makes me feel better. We'll talk more when I get there day after tomorrow." His voice held more enthusiasm.

"Before you go, I want to tell you something."

"Uh oh." I heard the smile in his tone. "Have you been meddling in something you shouldn't?"

"Not entirely. But a situation has come up."

"Oh no, Sarah." I listened for anger or frustration in his voice but couldn't hear any. "Tell me everything."

"A teacher acquaintance of mine contacted me about a missing student. She's eleven years old, has missed three days of school, and her grandfather, who's the emergency contact person, won't let anyone see her."

"Where are the parents?"

"In Reno. The mother is having some kind of medical issue, and the father is staying with her."

"Wait. Is the kid missing or just kept at home?"

"No one's sure yet. There's not enough to file a missing person report. In fact, in telling you this, I'm not so sure she is missing."

"What makes you suspicious?" He knew me well enough to know that I act on my suspicions, especially when a child could be at risk.

"The grandfather is incredibly evasive. He denies there's anything wrong and refuses to accept schoolwork from the teacher. He was hostile to me when I spoke to him this morning."

"You can request a missing person report, but I doubt you'll get much satisfaction. Given the info you've told me, there's nothing to warrant her being at risk."

"I'm not quite done yet." I heard him suck a breath in between clenched teeth. "Yesterday, while I was soliciting for the Christmas Fair, I talked to a lady who runs a clothing store that this missing girl and her mother go to. She told me Maddie, that's her name, was in the shop yesterday, minus her mom. Then she told me she got picked up by someone in a black Dodge Challenger."

"And..."

"This morning, I bought a cup of coffee for Kelly and told him everything."

"Good move."

"While we were talking, he got a call of a suspicious vehicle out on Mumy Lane."

"Don't tell me... a black Dodge Challenger."

"Yes."

"Was it occupied?"

"No. But Kelly found a gun under the driver's seat. And this is the worst—there was blood on the passenger dashboard."

Jake blew out an exasperated breath. "So now, at least, law enforcement can contact the grandfather for photos and information to make her a missing juvenile at risk. Right?"

"I'm sure Kelly is doing whatever is correct procedure. He took it seriously enough to call out the detectives. Someone said an evidence tech was on the way." I paused a heartbeat, knowing he waited for me to finish the story. "I went back to Layers. The grandfather's business is next door—you know the coin shop?"

"You mean the pawnshop?"

I guess I was the only one in town who didn't know High Sierra Coin and Collectibles was a darn pawnshop. "Yes, that one. Anyway, I banged on the door until he answered. He was uncooperative and hostile."

Jake scoffed. "He doesn't need to cooperate with you. You've got no authority to ask questions about his granddaughter. I don't know that I'd act any different."

I sighed, sounding defeated. "I know. You're right. I just got so mad, you know? Seeing that blood on the dashboard and figuring that it could be Maddie's, I had to do something."

"Thanks for telling me everything, Sarah. I know it wasn't easy. You like to play your information close to the vest. This is a good start to keeping our communication lines open over this distance."

After I said goodbye, it occurred to me that this conversation was one I'd dreaded. I was curious and didn't respect other people's boundaries all the time. Jake didn't appreciate that, but he'd asked for honesty.

And that's what I gave him. It was a much better ending to the day than I'd expected.

## Chapter Fifteen

It was Saturday, the day of the Christmas Parade. Tom and Anna had volunteered their horses and a wagon to advertise for the Christmas Fair. The only hitch was I had to drive the wagon. I was out of practice, but I figured a quick refresher should do the trick. My aunt and uncle did the heavy lifting—hauling the horses and a farm wagon normally used as a cook wagon. They tacked the animals up, thank goodness. I was sure I'd forgotten how. Paula had a sign maker draw up a pair of banners to attach to each side of the wagon to advertise the Christmas Fair. Of course, it included appropriate recognition to the Gibsons for the donation.

A pair of Belgians named Ed and Mike, would do the hauling. Tom had stored the wagon down at an empty warehouse near the canal. It gave the moms plenty of time to do their Christmas decorating magic. Mom and Anna talked about having the best float in the parade and had great fun decking out the wagon. It was a hoot watching them planning and executing their ideas. The project went something like this: For the parade, Tom—

dressed as Santa—would sit on a hay bale waving to kids while Anna—wearing a Missus Claus getup—would toss candy canes to the crowd. Mister and Missus Claus would have festively wrapped boxes with big bows surrounding them. Mark even volunteered to set up an iPhone with speakers to play Christmas carols. I would drive.

The horses Tom chose to haul the wagon were an experienced pair who worked well in synchrony. They'd worked in parades, done some farm work, and even been in a couple of movies. They were mature and settled, so I expected no funny business.

Today at the warehouse parking lot, Tom had hooked the horses up to the wagon for a dry run and review of my driving skills. Mom and Anna helped tack up Ed and Mike, who waited patiently. Mom painted their hooves with mineral oil to give them a nice shine, then gave Tom and me a thumbs-up signal. The pair of them retreated to the open warehouse door and waited. They'd finish decorating the wagon when my rehearsal was over.

With just a minor case of the jitters, I climbed up onto the bench seat. Tom had already reviewed the voice commands. He handed me the lines and whip. Ed and Mike were well-trained. They worked like one horse, and I had no difficulty remembering how to tug on the lines, when and where to tap with the whip, or when a voice command was needed. We wheeled around in the huge parking lot doing figure eights, circles, starts, and stops until I hollered at my uncle. "Tom. I'm comfortable with this."

I slid off the bench, handing the leads to my uncle as my aunt and mom began to unhook the horses. It was another four hours until the parade. Anna rebuffed my offer to stay and help finish the wagon. "You're not taking any credit for this masterpiece. Your mom and I have this well in hand. Go. Take a nap or something."

I laughed at the idea. Nap. Hmm. Not in the cards today. Jake was due to arrive in the next couple of hours. Rusty and I walked over to Layers. The yeasty smell told me that Charlie was working on his Christmas breads and rolls. He'd be working an extra couple of hours until after New Year's.

I stashed Rusty in the office, where he dropped onto his bed and promptly fell asleep. A nap was certainly in Rusty's cards. Javier had sent me November's books. After a half hour of studying them, I thanked God for Javier. Melody had begun the business with books and ledgers, which I continued. With Javier's elevation to manager, he'd selected and purchased a bakery software that kept track of all outgoing orders, supplies, and point-of-sale transactions. He'd even bought an add-on, a payroll feature to keep track of hours, pay, taxes, and deductions. After a steep learning curve, I was amazed that it took us so long to upgrade. He even projected the loan on our now completed café expansion would be paid off by this time next year.

I stood and stretched. Rusty lifted his head and dropped back down to sleep. Jake texted that he had arrived at Wesley's and would be in Bishop at four o'clock. With a glance out the window, I inspected my neighborhood, mostly rooftops and an alley or two. The weather was certainly cooperating with the parade— sunny, crisp, and cool, with a moderate air temperature to please everyone.

The low rumble announced someone sliding an aluminum garage door open. That would be to my left and behind Layers building, the vacant mechanic shop. A car started up. I looked out the window. The white

Lincoln Navigator pulled out of the building and into the alley. Norman Escher got out of the SUV, pulled the door shut, and drove down South Warren.

I looked at the time on my phone. I had to be at the warehouse at three thirty, and Jake would be there soon. I woke Rusty up and snapped on his leash. We flew down the stairs and out the back door. I looked around as the door closed behind me, letting Rusty sniff for places to irrigate.

The fall breeze was refreshing with a hint of rabbit-brush. Rusty wandered and peed his way to the mechanic's building. At the back door, I found the lock, a simple combination type with a thick hasp. I couldn't get past that. Rusty and I walked the perimeter of the building. As we rounded the last corner, I saw a window that faced the coin shop. Obscured by dust and grime, it was impossible to see inside.

As I had on the other two sliding windows, I pushed a corner of the glass. This window had a slight gap from the frame. A gentle shove sideways, and I had an open window. The glass on all the windows was clouded with years of dust and grime. It was dark inside, but I saw the Celica parked against a wall. I debated. What to do with Rusty if I decided to hop into the garage?

Simple. Rusty and I trotted back to the bakery and up the stairs. I unhooked the leash and gave him a *wait* command that was unnecessary. He flopped onto his bed for his afternoon nap as I hurried down the stairs. The kitchen clock read two o'clock. I had time, but not much. With a flashlight in my hand, I closed the door behind me and made for the garage.

# Chapter Sixteen

The window slid open just as easily as before. Using a canister ashtray left next to the back door of the pawnshop, I boosted myself up and over the window track. It opened to a worn workbench, covered with desert dust blown in through the gap in the window.

With nothing on the surface to obstruct me, I scooted inside. Dropping down to the dusty floor, I brushed the dust from my hands and scanned inside. Nothing but the Celica. The flashlight beam searched the interior for an office or a room where a kidnapped eleven-year-old could be hidden. Nothing.

A dead end.

Or was it? The Celica was unlocked. Of course. Why would Norman lock a vehicle inside a locked garage? I opened the driver-side door, and the musty smell of hours on the road, fast-food wrappers, gas station receipts, and an old wool blanket greeted me. I didn't want to touch anything inside.

Again, the flashlight beam searched the floor and walls for something to work with. A tire iron lay on the concrete floor accumulating dust. In seconds, I had it in my hand. Leaning inside the car, I caught the edge of the blanket with a spoke of the tire iron. I lifted the blanket but found nothing.

Except blood. The exposed underside released the coppery smell of blood. Enough blood to make me drop the tire iron when I jumped back. I straightened, then backed to the workbench, leaning on it to steady my breathing. I tried not to touch anything that I hadn't already. What to do now?

I couldn't call the police. I was trespassing, no matter who owned the building. I didn't dare endanger my chances to get the court reporter job by a trespassing citation—or worse. I had my phone.

Quickly and silently, I crossed the room to the Celica. The door stood open, and I considered where to begin. Using the photo app, I switched to video and captured an overview of the interior. I switched back to the photo function and leaned into the passenger side. Gas receipts sat on the leather seat, some wadded up, others not. The distance between gas stations was significant. From the southern end of Inyo County at Pearsonville, to Bishop, then Gardnerville, Nevada, just over the California/Nevada border.

To get a better vantage point, I went to the passenger side and opened the door. A small letter envelope fell out of the door's side pocket. I picked it up from the floor and, trying to keep my fingers on the edges, leafed through the contents.

Bank receipts, at least a dozen of them, from different banks in different communities. All showed large sums in the neighborhood of nine thousand dollars and eighty-five hundred dollars. The amounts varied, but none were over ten thousand. I knew that was significant but couldn't remember why.

The dates were all this week. The hair stood up on my arms. There was no way High Sierra Coin and Collectibles generated those amounts of revenue. Where did the money come from? My first instinct was to consider money laundering because of the amounts—all under the federal reporting requirements of ten thousand dollars per deposit. The other factor was the multiple banking institutions spread out over the area.

I closed the car doors carefully with my toe, dropped the tire iron where I'd found it, and made for the window. I took a deep breath, hoisted myself up, and swung my feet out to the alley. Using a fingertip, I slid the window into the same position I found it.

Back at Layers, I sat at the worktable. The bakers were gone for the day, and Javier was busy with customers at the front counter. I was alone in the kitchen and had to decide what direction to take. Whatever Norman's activity, it was out of my pay grade. I'd need to tell Frank about this and take my chances on a trespassing charge. With that thought, I texted him with a request to meet him after the parade. There was too much at stake.

I didn't know what was going on, but one thing was clear. Norman Escher was involved in a high-risk activity that I suspected put his granddaughter at risk. It scared the daylights out of me, wondering whose blood was on the blanket.

# *Chapter Seventeen*

I sat in the kitchen until the last minute. Rusty and I trotted the six blocks to the warehouse. Ed and Mike were hitched up and stood patiently. They didn't seem to mind the elf hats between their ears or the sleigh bells on their surcingle. The bells jingled at the slightest movement, but the pair kept their calm. Tom, on the other hand, was a bit anxious. He looked at his watch and glared at me.

Putting Rusty in the seat next to where I'd be, I said to Tom, "You said you wanted me here at three-thirty. It's just three-twenty-five now."

Mom came out of the building with a Christmas cowgirl apron and chaps. "Here, put these on."

A glance is all I needed. "Not a chance. Who wears chaps on a wagon? Besides, I want to wear my Layers Bakery shirt."

Mom shrugged. "Okay, then. I guess you're ready." Tom had his Santa suit and beard on. If Melody had been here, I was sure she would've been dressed up as an elf and tossed candy canes to kids in the crowd. How I missed her.

Tom switched on the Christmas tree lights and helped Anna get up on the wagon. She made a homey Missus Claus. She tapped at her phone, and soon *Silent Night* blared through the afternoon. Ironic, I thought.

The staging area was seven blocks away, a mere block from the bakery. I gathered up the lines, clicking my tongue in a distinctively horsey cue. "Git up."

Ed and Mike knew the drill. They stepped forward, their heads bobbing in unison and their bells jingling. They plodded on without a complaint about the lighted wreaths around their necks, elf hats, and darn jingle bells. When I told them to "haw," they did what they were supposed to do—turn left. They ambled the three blocks down South Second Street to East South Street. We continued at an easy pace until we approached South Main Street. Another "haw" turn, and we were within a block of the staging area. I held up the team and waited for the parade director to confirm our place in line. We were in the right place, so we waited.

I reached into my back pocket for my phone. Four twenty. Ten minutes until showtime. And no answer from Frank. He was busy with the crowd, surely. With a small-town police department like Bishop's, an event like the Christmas Parade required all-hands-on-deck.

"What the..." Anna's voice rose above the words to Bing Crosby's honeyed tones of "White Christmas." A distant crash made Ed and Mike's ears swivel in that direction. It was toward Layers. I followed the focus of their attention and heard an engine powering down Lagoon Street from South Warren. Ed and Mike stood dutifully still.

The Lincoln Navigator. Norman Escher looked tiny

behind the wheel of the huge SUV. But he drove like the Incredible Hulk. With tires screeching, the Navigator turned to the right and headed south out of town on Main Street, which was called Highway 395. The vehicle bumped a portable barricade and accelerated on his way.

Although it attracted plenty of attention, all the law enforcement was tied up with parade traffic control. Other than speeding, he hadn't done anything to warrant police or California Highway Patrol interest.

I held my breath as I counted the time from when I left the garage until now. Norman had been gone when I went in but must have returned soon after I left. I could only speculate on his urgency, but I crossed my fingers that he hadn't seen me. I was certain I'd left everything as I'd found it.

I hoped he hadn't figured out I'd been in there.

# Chapter Eighteen

After the parade, we drove the wagon back to the warehouse where the trailers were stored. Although the streetlights were on, I was grateful for the blinking Christmas lights on the wagon along the way. I helped untack 'the boys' as Tom called them. A couple of sugar cubes won me their eternal affection. They'd done an excellent job. They'd even spent some time at City Park getting their velvety noses rubbed by kids. Children's bright, astonished eyes took in the sweet behemoths. Babies, toddlers, and kindergartners oohed and aahed at Ed and Mike's size. Parents smiled with gratitude for the boys' gentleness. I felt a twinge of envy at the family scenes but savored the moments just the same.

Two hours later, when the horse and wagon trailers were mere taillights on Main Street, I texted Jake. *All done with parade. You around?*

His reply was quick. *Meet me at the Bishop PD booth in the park.*

Mom gave me a lift to the park. Dropping me off, she

remarked, "It was fun, wasn't it?"

I leaned in and gave her a kiss on the cheek. "More fun than I expected."

"Good. You'll do it again next year. Anna and I had a blast putting all those decorations together. Oh, by the way, we decided that Anna will do the Christmas Eve gathering, and we'll do the brunch on Christmas Day."

"Sounds good to me. I'll help wherever I'm needed."

"I know, sweetheart." With that, she was off to help the Gibsons with their horses.

I walked through the park, the evening fair for December but sweater weather. Crowds meandered through the booths of crafts, wines, assorted nuts, and plenty of garage-made jewelry. The sun set earlier, yet everyone was filled with holiday spirit. Families with children, mature couples holding hands, and every now and then, an elf. Or a Missus Clause doppelganger handing out candy. Santa was in the gazebo listening to little children's dreams.

I felt wistful as I wondered if I'd ever have to wipe chocolate from a pair of rosebud lips.

Jake and Frank stood beside the Bishop PD booth with a third man who looked vaguely familiar. The Explorer Post was a cadre of high school students with law enforcement aspirations who staffed the booth with crime prevention, bicycle safety, and car-seat-fitting material. Stacks of multi-colored handouts on the counter waited for interested parties.

Jake spotted me first and waved as I walked toward him. He moved around the corner out of Frank's line of sight. I grabbed Jake's arm and planted a kiss on his lips, surprising him. And surprising me too. He recovered first and swung an arm around my waist.

I laughed. "Not too close. I smell like horses." That

horse smell was heaven to me, but nonriders never really got it. Except Jake. He nuzzled my hair and breathed into it.

Frank cleared his throat. "Sarah and Jake. Can you come here for a moment?"

Jake held my hand when we faced Frank and the man beside him, a man around my age with curly brown hair and glasses. He wore the Bishop winter uniform—a puffy jacket and jeans.

"Sarah Murray and Jake Charters. I'd like you to meet Will Hall."

"Hall? Are you Madison's father?" My stomach flipped, thinking about the troubles in store for this man. "How is your wife?"

"She's doing better, thanks for asking." He toed a piece of caramel popcorn on the grass. "And yes, I'm Madison's dad. Do you know where she is?"

I blew out the breath I'd been holding. "No. I was hoping you might know. Is there a missing person report on her yet?"

Frank answered. "No. Mr. Hall just arrived from Reno. One of his neighbors told him to get hold of me, and here we are. I have a beat officer coming to take a report." Frank eyed me. "I told Mr. Hall that you'd been looking around after Maddie."

"Yes. I have. And there's more information now." I looked around at the crowd. Christmas joy was everywhere, from sugar-saturated kids to moms and dads busy chasing them, all had sparkles in their eyes.

Jake caught my glance. "It's too noisy here. Why don't we all go to the police station? Mister Hall can make a report, and we can catch up with some privacy."

Frank nodded. "Good idea. I'll have the patrol officer meet us there for the report."

# Chapter Nineteen

Sitting in the quiet of the police chief's office, I dreaded what was coming. Frank sat behind his desk with Mister Hall and me across from him. Jake leaned against the wall.

Frank suggested he fill Mister Hall in with the basic information we had so far. Kelly had told me he would brief Frank as well as Jake. I didn't want to risk telling Mister Hall something that would cause him any more concern, so I was more than happy to let Frank do the talking. After Mister Hall left, I'd fill Frank and Jake in on what I'd found.

Mister Hall leaned in and slammed a fist on the desk. "That louse Norman. I knew it wasn't a good idea to leave Maddie with him."

"Any particular reason? Has he done something to jeopardize her safety before?" Jake spoke for the first time.

"Not really." The man's face twisted with anxiety. "He just doesn't make good decisions. He's made some real bad choices in the past few years." His eyes pleaded with Frank and Jake not to condemn him. "We were stuck. I had to be with my wife in Reno. It was life-threatening, you know. I left Maddie with her granddad because she didn't need to see her mother dying."

The patrol officer tapped on the door, announcing he was ready to take Mister Hall's missing person report. Hall got up and followed the officer.

Jake closed the door behind him.

Frank asked, "Now, Sarah, you said you have some new information?"

"Boy, do I." I studied Jake, knowing he wouldn't approve of my detective moves. But there was something very big going on here. "I know you both will be unhappy with me, but I found some things that need further checking."

Frank urged me on. "Okay, Sherlock, fill us in."

"I saw Norman Escher leave in his big Lincoln. He stores it in the empty garage next to Layers Bakery. I figured he'd be out for a while, and I found an open window. I crawled in."

"Sarah, what were you thinking?" Jake launched himself off the wall. "You could've..."

I held up my hand. "Wait. You need to hear this. Then you can chew me out." I fixed my gaze on Frank. I didn't care as much about his reaction. "Norman's old car, the blue Celica, was inside. I took a video when I looked around. I'll show you in a minute. Then I checked out the car. It's a hatchback, so I looked behind the driver's seat. I found a blanket with blood on it. Lots of blood."

"Oh, my Lord." Jake's incredulous response was more at my nerve than surprise at the blanket.

"That's not all. On the passenger side was a bunch of receipts. Gas receipts from Ridgecrest to Gardnerville."

Jake was thoughtful. "All along Highway 395."

"In the side pocket of the passenger door was an envelope with a dozen bank deposit receipts. All the same day at different banks and all under ten thousand dollars."

Frank whistled.

"Do you have more to tell us?" Jake was angry. I heard it in the tone of his voice.

I sighed. "Just one more little thing. While I was waiting at the staging area with the wagon, I saw the Lincoln leave southbound in a hurry."

The two men were silent for a moment. Frank spoke first. "The dad doesn't need to know any of this yet. But with the blood on that blanket, it could be too late for the little girl."

"Let's ask him if Norman has any place he'd stash her to keep her safe. We don't have to tell him why." Jake's brows drew together. He'd told me before. He didn't like lying, but there were times when strategies depended on what people knew and what they didn't.

Frank stood, opened the door to his office, and yelled for the officer taking the report. "When you're done with the report information, I'd like you and Mister Hall to meet me in my office."

"Yessir. Just finished for now. We'll be right in."

Frank caught Mister Hall at the door. "Is there any place you can think of where Norman would put Maddie to keep her safe?"

"Safe? What're you talking about?"

"Norman may have believed Maddie was at risk from some criminal elements."

Mister Hall shrank back. "Criminal elements? In Bishop?"

Jake took over. "Is there a place or a person Norman

would leave her with? Is there a relative's house, barn, or shed he had access to?"

"No. Nothing I can think of. My brain is so scrambled right now, I can't think." His red-rimmed eyes searched our faces. "I haven't gotten any sleep in four days. I'm surprised I made it here from Reno without driving into a tree."

At Frank's nod, the officer took Mister Hall by the elbow. "Go on home, now, Mister Hall. We'll call you as soon as we hear anything."

When we heard the front door close and lock, Frank yelled to the patrol officer. "Patrick, come on in here. We need to update you with some info about this case."

## Chapter Twenty

They didn't kick me out for Patrick's briefing. I didn't find out anything new but felt a bit honored that they let me stay and reported what I'd found.

Frank concluded with his direction. "I want a full-court press with this missing juvenile at risk. I want a media release, posters, and we'll do a door-to-door in her neighborhood tomorrow."

Jake had a question. "Where does Norman live? We could do door-to-door in that neighborhood too."

Frank fired up his department computer. "All we have is a post office box, no physical address."

"I wouldn't be surprised if he slept in the store." I'd seen him coming and going at odd hours. I wondered why I hadn't figured that out before.

"What about a search warrant for the pawnshop?"

"Good idea. I'll get Patrick to work on it tonight and see if we can find a judge early tomorrow morning."

We stood. Jake and Frank shook hands. "Jake, I want to remind you that I've got a trip planned for Maui over Christmas. I'll be back for New Year's."

Jake steered me through the back door before I could question why Frank would report his time off to Jake. "I'll drive you back to your car. Is it at the bakery?"

I nodded. We rode in silence to the Layers parking lot.

"Sarah," Jake left the engine on but put the SUV in park. "I'm having a really tough time with you being in the middle of investigations. The first two were murders, and this very well could be. I've got a lot of things going on right now, and I don't want to have to worry about you."

I chewed my lip, considering what to say. "It's best you find out about me before we make any long-term commitments." I swallowed. Was I cutting off the best person that ever happened to me?

"So, you're saying that this isn't an anomaly? You plan on continuing this?"

I shrugged. I felt bad that it looked like I dismissed his concerns so casually. I had to say something. "Jake, I can't say I'll be in the middle of every police inquiry. I don't intend to. People reach out to me, and I hate turning away someone in trouble."

His sigh blew out all his breath. "It's so dangerous. I cannot lose another woman that I love."

"I understand. We should take some time apart to think this whole adventure over."

He was silent for a minute as we got out of his SUV, dread looming in my heart. "Maybe we need to do that."

# Chapter Twenty-One

Rusty practically had his legs crossed when I picked him up from the office. He'd been locked up for far too many hours. We made it through the back door, and he peed on the first post he found. Poor guy. He would be hungry, too, and it was time to take him back to Mom and Dad's.

I leaned against the stucco building letting the leash run through my fingers. A sob rose in my throat. I was unable to stop it. What had I done? Why did I believe that I could do a better job than a police officer? How could I jeopardize my future with Jake? He was a wonderful guy. Handsome, compassionate, professional, and a lot of other things I couldn't name right now.

I was a fool. I'd better figure a way out of this mess, or I was going to lose him. Using my sweatshirt cuff to dry my eyes, I glanced around for Rusty. It was dark, and the streetlights didn't reach this corner of the bakery where it butted up against the garage and the pawnshop. My flashlight was still in my pocket, so I retrieved it and flipped it on. I called out for him. I heard his dog tags clanging together around the corner.

Rusty had a leg hiked on a canister-style ashtray next to the door at the back of the pawnshop—the one I'd used to get through the window of the garage. I sighed, glancing around the building, hoping Norman didn't see Rusty. I sniffled, wishing I had a tissue. I walked over, trying to catch the leash near the wet patch on the ashtray, just as Rusty knocked the canister sideways. It didn't fall but rocked it enough to uncover a key.

Oh. My. Lord. This is just the situation Jake found so troubling. On the other hand, I have a key to a building that I suspect has something to do with the kidnapping of a little girl. Why wouldn't I go in?

I took a deep breath and unlocked the steel security door. I found it odd that Norman had bars installed on the exterior of his building yet kept a key in such an obvious place.

The key flipped the lock open with a quiet snick. I paused, sure that sound had been heard all over south Bishop. No sirens or alarms. The door swung open, releasing a foul, musty smell of old cigarette smoke.

With Rusty beside me and the flashlight in hand, I tiptoed through what looked like a back room. It held a rumpled cot and nightstand. I was right. Norman did live here. Next to it sat a small surplus-type desk piled with two boxes, books, and binders. I'd look at that later. First, I wanted to be sure Maddie wasn't here.

Nothing stirred. With a loud whisper, I called out. "Maddie?"

Nothing.

I walked through a canvas-type fabric curtain to the store. Collectibles certainly was a catch-all word for what he had on display. I'd seen similar stuff in a senior village garage sale back in LA. Betty Boop and Kewpie dolls had their own shelf. Old Disney characters on the next two shelves, and armed forces memorabilia had a whole rack, next to the collection of old telephones and televisions. All of it covered in dust.

None of the merchandise would generate funds such as Norman had deposited recently.

Now the papers on the desk seemed more important. I let Rusty sniff around, but he seemed bored after a few minutes. At the desk, I put the flashlight between my teeth and used both hands to skim over the papers. The binders held catalogs of antiques and collectibles. The books were references for art history. I snorted, thinking about any of the items I'd seen as art. The first box held unpacked statuettes and figurines. I looked through the top layer of items. Again, I saw nothing of any value.

The second box held the same, except for an envelope similar to the one in the Celica's passenger-side door. Receipts from a company called Anchorman Holdings with an address in Lancaster, California. Lancaster was a high desert community on the fringes of the Los Angeles commute. I leafed through the dozen receipts. The amounts were enormous, well over the total of the bank receipts. The note on top showed Norman had been paid forty-eight thousand dollars this past week. The totals were in the range of two hundred thousand dollars this month alone.

But for what?

# Chapter Twenty-Two

Sunday morning, my alarm went off a bit later than on workdays. Church.

I couldn't get out of it. My whole family would be attending, Tom and Anna, as well as my mother and father. Mark? Well, Mark was Mark. Her cousin, Tom and Anna's son, wouldn't be attending.

Pastor Wesley Charters would conduct the service at the New Life Fellowship church. Chances were his brother, Jake Charters, would also be attending. I knew it would be awkward, but I couldn't duck seeing him forever. I showered and dressed in an outfit I wore regularly for work in the courtroom, a dress and jacket. I even carried a purse instead of a backpack. My, how my life had changed since moving back to Bishop.

I couldn't help but notice that Jake sat in the back during the service. I tried not to look for him, but I caught his eye more than once. The third time, I got a rueful smile. I didn't look anymore.

We filed out after the service. Mom and Dad planned on a big breakfast at home with Tom and Anna. I'd been included since I live with them, but I didn't really feel like socializing. I was thinking over rationalizations for how I could beg off when Emily grabbed my arm.

"Hey, girl. You free for brunch?"

I faced her, an infant in her arms and filled with expectation.

"Uh, I don't know. Mom and Dad are having a big breakfast at home..."

"You can see them anytime, Sarah. You live with them. Maybe you need a break. Let's go to Mack's. You love their pancakes."

Yes, I did. I loved sugary sweet breakfasts, pancakes with real maple syrup being my favorite. I'd become a connoisseur of pancakes, and Mack's was the best anywhere. Breakfast for me was usually fruit or granola brought from home. "All right. You talked me into it."

Even with the Sunday after-church rush, we were able to get a table for three adults and four children with no problems. We started with coffee, thank goodness, as I'd missed my morning cup at home.

"Wes had a wonderful message this morning, didn't you think?" Emily stirred milk into her coffee, then wiped the baby's chin, all in one fluid movement. I'd have to be an octopus to manage what she just did without thinking.

My mind had wandered during his homily. "Refresh my memory."

"Daydreaming during church?" She slapped my hand playfully. "Be thankful for what you have. That message coming from that man was enormously powerful."

"Oh, yes." I stared into my black coffee.

"I mean, he's lost so much over his lifetime but especially this past year. The numbers in the congregation fell for a while, but now they're up again, better than ever. He didn't say it today, but he's told Matt that he's sure it's related to Melody's death."

He'd almost lost the house they'd lived in too. Money had been a problem. It took a big heart and soul to thank God for the blessings he found after his wife's death. I was glad he'd found some solace after being arrested for her murder. I loved Wesley for a long time, as the brother I'd never had.

Number two son jumped on the banquette seat next to Emily, and she calmly shook her head. She'd said he was six years old, but he sat, pulling a napkin under his chin. One-handedly, Em tucked the napkin into her young son's shirt. He looked around expectantly. "Milk? Panacakes?"

"They're coming, Noah. You have to wait for the cook to make them."

The boy nodded solemnly and sat back. Matt wrangled the other two, a boy and a girl, got them ready for a meal, and ordered breakfast for the whole family. He let me order my own.

When the food came, Matt took the baby and sat her in the highchair. The three others managed with his help. He must have known Em had something to tell me and kept all the kids out of her way until it was done.

Emily grinned, her pride shining through. "Not very subtle, is he?"

"Nope, but he's a great dad."

She nodded emphatically as she dug into her eggs Benedict. "I did good, didn't I?"

"Yes, you did."

"Which brings me to this question. Are you or are you not seeing Jake Charters?"

I tried not to sigh or sound pathetic. "As of last night, we're taking a break."

Emily's fork clattered to the plate. "Are you kidding me?"

"I wish I was."

She pushed her plate away, her red curls shaking with energy. "You're going to let the best thing that ever happened to you slip away?"

"I knew you'd be angry."

She sat back against the upholstered booth, her lower lip stuck out like a three-year-old. "I am."

"We're taking a break from each other to figure some things out."

Her round face hardened. "Like what?"

"He's a widower, and he's afraid my snooping is going to get me in trouble, maybe even killed. He says he couldn't lose another woman he loved."

"He said that?" She eyed me, scrutinizing my soul. "He loves you. Do you love him?"

"Yes." My pancakes had gotten cold and doughy. I dropped my fork on the table.

"Why the devil are you keeping up the detective work?"

"I wish I knew. I just hate not helping people in need. Like this missing girl, Maddie."

"Oh yeah, I heard about her on the radio this morning. What are you doing about that?"

"Nothing specific. Mostly just keeping my eyes open. Her grandfather's shop is right beside Layers."

She crossed her arms. "Well, that's not dangerous. I don't know what he's so upset about."

"It's problematic." This wasn't the place to tell her all I'd done. "I appreciate your support, Emily. I hope we figure this out. It's complicated by the fact that he lives three hundred and fifty miles away."

Her head tipped toward me, indicating something important was on its way. "You need to make this right. He shouldn't be the one who got away. He's a great guy, and you deserve each other. Besides that, you need babies."

I sighed. She was right. I needed to make it work between Jake and me. It wasn't just because I wanted a family, but I wanted him for my partner—for life.

In the restaurant parking lot after breakfast, I hugged Emily and Matt, ignoring the drool on his shoulder. These two made me happy. They gave me hope that maybe someday, I could have a slice of what they had.

I got in my car and pulled out my phone. Frank had sent a text about stopping by the police department and picking up fliers for Maddie. I'd agreed as it would fit nicely into my contacts about the Christmas Fair. I was talking to so many people during the day that passing out fliers would be an easy task.

Then, I'd go home and change into jeans. I'd look in on Tom and Anna to see if they needed any help with Ed and Mike.

## Chapter Twenty-Three

D ad was waiting for me when Rusty and I got back from Anna's. Ed and Mike were groomed and beautiful. Their shoer had called to move up their shoeing date to today. He had to go out of town for the holidays, and some animals couldn't wait to be shoed. Because they were working a special Christmas sleigh event in Mammoth, he'd work on a Sunday to get them done. It wasn't normal, but it didn't create any problems. I stood by with them so Anna and Tom didn't have to. I loved their massive size and gentle nature. I couldn't resist a gentle stroke on a velvety muzzle.

"Hey, Dad."

His newspaper was folded neatly beside him on an end table next to his recliner. "Hi, darlin'. What d'you say about sitting down and passing the time of day with your old dad?"

"I'd love to. Let me change first. I'm dirty from horses." I opened the back door for Rusty, and he trotted out to Mom in the garden.

"No worries. Your Momma doesn't care if the sofa smells like that." He squinted at me. "To tell you the truth, I think she kind of likes it."

"Okay." I plopped onto the sofa and sunk into the pillows. If she didn't like the smell I brought with me, she'd have the upholstery cleaned. Mom had exquisite taste, and yet the house was never what I considered *decorated*. Everything had a function, even if the point was pictures to remind us of days past.

Except at Christmas. Mom *decorated* the Murray house from top to bottom, inside and out. It began as you opened the door. The sweet cinnamon, cloves, and orange peel smell wafted through the house all day. Mom had the potpourri simmering in a small crockpot in the kitchen. Holly and evergreen garlands draped every arched surface. Several framed pictures had been removed, wrapped like spectacular Christmas gifts, and rehung. Candy cane embroidered towels awaited guests in the bathroom and every table—small and large—had a centerpiece.

The main spectacle inside was the living room Christmas tree. Ornaments were little glass globes of memories from my childhood, family trips, and gifts from friends. While I always thought Mom preferred the delicate Victorian Christmas style, what she designed was a vintage all-American, homey charm that recalled holidays of years past. I always felt that as a family, our hearts were fullest when celebrating Christmas together.

Dad's responsibility was the exterior, under Mom's supervision, of course. Lights and the almost life-sized crèche had been set up, so Dad took a day off.

"I noticed you haven't brought your friend Jake by for a while." Just like a Murray. Get right to the point.

"Well, Dad, we're taking a break for a while. We need to figure some things out before we make a commitment to a future."

"That sounds serious."

"It is. He's worried about me. He wants me to stop asking questions when something isn't right. He's afraid because he lost his first wife."

"Well, he has a point." I knew Dad's perspective was similar to Jake's. As a parent, he hated that I put myself in places that weren't safe. I'd done that twice in the past six months and scared both my parents.

"I know. It's not something I do without thinking, Dad. I'm cautious."

"You're helping with this missing little girl?"

I splayed my hands out, palms up. "I don't know if I'm helping. But I'm passing out fliers and talking to people while out on the Christmas Fair rounds."

"That doesn't sound dangerous. What's he want, then?"

"You know, Dad. I'm not sure. We didn't get that far before the idea came around to splitting up."

"Well, honey, maybe you should find out what's on his mind. If he wants you to stop snooping into other people's business, that's one thing, but to stop helping people in need, that's another. Ignoring people who need help is just not how you were raised."

I sighed, realizing how ingrained in me the drive to help was. Dad was right. Maybe I should talk to Jake and see if we could meet in the middle.

"Thanks, Dad. You've helped me figure out a direction."

Still in his recliner, he reached out to me. I sank into his arms in a snuggle I hadn't enjoyed since, well, I couldn't remember when. I felt like I was twelve again when my beloved kitty, Roscoe, died. The understanding and compassion of this man had set the bar for my future relationships. I'd failed to use it as a gauge with Blaine, but Jake was another matter.

Now, I had to figure out what I'd say to him.

# Chapter Twenty-Four

J ake was ignoring my texts. I sent two of them, even though I knew he was on his way back to Petaluma. Talking over the phone wasn't optimum, but better than nothing. I still wasn't completely sure what I would say to him, but I couldn't let him go—at least without trying one more time.

In the meantime, Monday brought us a day closer to the Christmas Fair. With Rosalyn, Javier's sister-in-law, helping out front, I had some free time. I grabbed a stack of Christmas Fair fliers and an equal amount of Missing Maddie posters.

I started on the east side at the south end of town. The RV Storage Spot would have travelers from all different areas. Missing Maddie posters were welcomed and went in their front window. The next business was the district nine office of the state highway department known as Caltrans. Their employees traveled state roads all over the area, east to Death Valley and south to Kern County, and north beyond Bridgeport, almost to the Nevada border. My goal was to expose the workers to her plight and have them memorize little Maddie's face. With their radios, they could easily notify law enforcement if she was sighted.

The hardware store was next. There were plenty of customers coming and going. The store owner was happy to post several Maddie fliers in strategic places. Oh, and Christmas Fair fliers too.

As I walked Main Street, I was amazed at how many merchants and customers already knew about Maddie's disappearance. The local radio and television stations had been playing public service announcements. To my dismay, no one had seen her since Tuesday.

By noon, my feet were killing me. I crossed Main Street, intent on going directly back to the bakery. I stopped in at Mack's and got a chocolate milkshake to go. On my way out, a sheriff's patrol car passed. I couldn't tell who the driver was, but after it veered to a red zone on the corner of West Pine Street, I knew it was Kelly.

I saw a huge hand wave me over, and I bent down to see in the passenger window. My friend, Kelly, laughed. "You going back to the bakery?"

"What's so funny?"

"You." He nodded to the passenger seat. "Want a ride?"

"If you're offering. My feet are tired."

"Good timing then."

"You bet." The least I could do was buy him lunch at the café. "Had your lunch yet?"

"Yeah, about an hour ago." He glanced at his watch. "But I think it's donut thirty."

"I know just the place."

We found a table in the crowded café, and I ordered a salad. I felt a bit guilty with my milkshake, but no one seemed to notice. Kelly slurped a cup of black coffee as I polished off my salad. Rosalyn served him up a beautiful bear claw, nicely warmed. He dug in.

Between bites, he asked, "You want to hear about the car?"

"The car?" Which car, the Navigator, the Celica?

"The black Challenger on Mumy Road."

"Ah. Yes, I do."

"It's registered out of Lancaster, down south. The owner is a corporation, Anchorman Holdings."

I put down my milkshake. "I've got to tell you something. Promise you won't arrest me?"

Kelly's eyes widened just a bit. He wiped his mouth with a napkin, wadded it up, and tossed it on the empty plate. He knew me well enough to believe I wouldn't break the law, exactly. Maybe bend it a little. But this might put him in a tough position. It's why I didn't go to the police department with the information.

"Maybe. Tell me what you've got first, then I'll tell you whether you're in trouble or not."

"No way. Give me the get-out-of-jail-free card first. Then, I'll spill."

With a wry smile, he said, "Oh, go on. You hardly ever break the law."

Where to start? "Saturday night, I found a key to High Sierra Coins and Collectibles."

"Oh no. Don't tell me…"

"I walked in to be sure everything was okay. I actually thought Maddie might be inside, but she wasn't."

"Ah, jeez."

"In the office, I found some paperwork from

Anchorman Holdings. Documentation that they gave Norman Escher a significant amount of money."

"What kind of amount are we talking about?"

"I didn't take the time to total it, but I'm guessing it's in the two-hundred-thousand-dollar range, just for this month."

Kelly's jaw dropped. "I'll pass this on to Quentin. He may want to talk to you. He'll need to know how you got into the business."

"Sure." I sounded confident, but in the back of my mind, I worried about jeopardizing my court job. "Did you check around the Mumy Lane area for anyone who might've heard a gunshot?"

"Yeah, but didn't get anywhere. There's a big horse boarding facility down the road. They all said they heard gunshots off and on all day because it's pheasant season. So I checked. It is."

"Thanks for the bear claw." Kelly stood, brushing bits of dough and sugar off his uniform pants. "I'm sure you'll be hearing from Quentin soon."

"One more thing," I said, and Kelly rolled his eyes.

"You might get word to the PD officer that they don't need a search warrant for the coin shop to find Maddie. They might want one for the paperwork."

He nodded. "Remember, Quentin will be contacting you."

I knew I would.

# Chapter Twenty-Five

later that afternoon, Libby texted me to bring both fliers to her at her new digs. She'd rented a duplex on West Elm Street, a quiet, well-established neighborhood. It was a charming old place with arched portals and a built-in cupboard inside. Outside, a set of French doors opened to a backyard with a nice lawn. The neighboring unit was vacant, but the landlord told Libby that the new tenant would be moving in soon.

Libby had made this little place a delightful home. I saw her in every corner. The memorabilia and tchotchkes from her parents' house were nowhere to be seen. The interior was clean and neat, almost Scandinavian in style. A few framed posters of rock and goth music groups graced the halls, but overall, it was a pleasant place.

"Every time I see this place, it's changed." I took the glass of iced tea she offered. "Thanks. You've made it more yours than the last time I was here."

"Yeah. It'll be a shame to give it up in January when I go to San Luis." She ran a hand over the old plaster walls. "I really feel at home here."

"I know that's something you've been seeking for a long time."

"Yep." She dropped into a blue Ikea club chair. "But also, I know that being with Cam is where my home is. So, I'll take all this with me and make a home there."

"No Christmas tree?"

"I've never been a big Christmas fan. Holidays around our house were nonevents." Her eyes dimmed with troubled memories. Then she focused on me. "But really, Cam and I decided to do Christmas next year when we're more settled. He'll be here, but he'll be studying and working with the vets."

Amazed at her resilience, I reached for her hand. She had small hands, as she was small in stature. But what she did with those hands was magic. The bakery had doubled its business in the past five months. The website helped with travelers, but locals used word of mouth to make the business succeed. She had a solid and loyal daily following. I gave her strict instructions to write down her recipes before she leaves. Marie and Charlie did a wonderful job, but Libby was an artist.

"Did you bring the posters?" Libby was ready to move onto the next subject.

I reached into my backpack and pulled out both sets. "Here you are. Thanks for spreading the word."

"The Christmas Fair is easy. Everyone expects to do some last-minute shopping at the fair. As for the girl..." Libby shook her head. "You weren't here when the grandfather got caught forging certificates for some of his collectibles. The stinker didn't even do jail time. But he cut his own throat. There are lots of coin collectors in Bishop. Military memorabilia too. He was the only game in town, so he had a pretty solid clientele, according to what my dad told me. Once he was arrested, locals went out of town because they couldn't trust him. They felt it was a real betrayal. A real scandal. Now it looks like there's something worse brewing for that family." Her face scrunched in a questioning expression. "What the heck could've happened to her?"

"No idea. But the longer she's gone, the worse the possibilities become." I leaned forward in my chair, wringing my hands. "I feel there's more I could be doing to find her."

Libby squinted. "Wait just a minute. You're caught between a rock and a hard place here. You've done everything you could possibly do as a civilian. Handing out these posters are as aggressive as you should be. There are reasons you can't do more. First, because you're not a cop. And second, any snooping you do will jeopardize your relationship with Jake."

I blew out an exasperated breath. "You're right, but..."

"No buts, Sarah. Your whole future depends on this."

First Emily, then Dad, and now Libby have told me to back off my snooping. How do I do that?

# Chapter Twenty-Six

Scandal. Scandal. The word kept echoing in my mind. I'd been in Los Angeles when Norman Escher's scandal had been discovered. I missed the news. But hearing about it now, I was sure it had a part to play in the whole missing Maddie case.

And Jake pulled at my attention too. How could I let him go?

I couldn't. I loved him. Despite the distance we had to work with, my life felt empty without him. He hadn't answered my texts. I decided to wait before I texted him again. He could be busy saving the world.

The next morning, I planned on hitting the downtown merchants with fliers. Rusty stayed at home with Mom. I spent the early hours at the bakery helping with the rush, then hit the sidewalks around ten o'clock. It had been a week since Maddie had last been seen.

I picked up where I'd left off yesterday. At the Bishop Creek Restaurant, beside the twinkling lights from a huge blue spruce Christmas tree, I took a few minutes to catch up with a few old friends from the Boulangerie

Bakery. I'd gotten to know them during the month I helped the owner salvage his bakery. The owner, Reginald Bateau, had fired all his employees in a temper tantrum just minutes before he was murdered. A handful of his staff had found work at Bishop Creek.

It was fun to catch up, but they were working, even if it was a slack time between breakfast and lunch. I cut my visit short and walked out into the brilliant early winter sunshine.

"Ma'am?"

I turned to find the hostess calling me. "Can I see that missing girl poster?"

"Sure." She could've seen it inside where I left three of them. Did she have something to say?

Blond and willowy, her polite manners made her the perfect person to greet clientele. Now, she inspected Maddie's photo. "Yes, I saw her."

My heart thumped in my chest. "When?"

"Tuesday, down there by the pawnshop." She handed the flier back to me.

"No, you keep it. What was she doing?"

"She was with two guys. One short guy—he looked like he was on steroids—in a black muscle car, newer model, and the other was a bald guy. He drove up with the girl in a black Dodge sedan. I saw the emblem. I don't know the model, but he pushed her out of it, and the roided-up guy hauled her into the muscle car. She didn't look happy, but I didn't really think much of it."

"Okay," I leaned in to read her name tag. "Cheri, you need to call the police department and tell them this."

"Oh, I can't. I'm working, and the manager doesn't like us not working..."

"Cheri, this is important. The police need to know."

She squinted into the morning sunlight. "You're sure?"

"Yes. I am. I'll stay here while you call them."

"I need to get inside."

"I'll follow you." I wanted to be sure she called.

She made the call and, after disconnecting, told me they were on their way. This was critical information. Who were the two men who obviously abducted Maddie? And why? Until now, I'd believed that Norman was operating on his own. Now, clearly, we knew he wasn't.

# Chapter Twenty-Seven

I waited long enough to see the patrol unit drive up to the restaurant. Reassured that the information would be passed along, I looked at my phone. Libby had messaged me. *I got a new neighbor, a cranky old man.*

*Are you at home now?*

*Yes, come on over.* I was far away enough from my car that I decided it made more sense to walk to her house. I'd pick up my car after seeing Libby. It seemed to me that she'd have more important things to do on her day off than commiserate with me.

It was noon by the time I knocked on Libby's screen. The day had warmed enough that she had her front door open.

Libby trotted to the door. "You've got to meet this guy. You're just not going to believe what a small world it is."

Small world?

Libby motioned me in, and I followed her through the house to the backyard. The fence separating the two yards was chain link. "What a nice yard, Libby."

"Yeah, it is. It would be great for a puppy." She flashed her big-eyed *poor me* look. "But I'm not going to be here that long."

Good decision. You never know what's on the other end of a journey until you get there. Libby and Cam might not be able to find an apartment that allows dogs.

She stood at the bottom of the stairs and leaned on the chain link. I waited at the top of the steps. "George, yoo-hoo. George."

Mystified by her behavior, I folded my arms across my chest.

"I'm coming. I'm coming. Hold your dang horses." I heard the shuffle of house slippers and the bump on the floor of a cane. A wizened old man sneaking up on his seventies appeared at the top of his stairs. His gray hair stood on end as if he'd been napping. Dressed in a flannel shirt and corduroy pants, he stood tall. George's eyes were a sharp, penetrating brown. I got the feeling he didn't miss much. I'd never met George, but he seemed so familiar.

"George, this is Sarah." Libby turned to me. "Sarah, this is my new neighbor, George Charters." She enunciated the last name so I wouldn't miss it.

"Wait. Charters? As in Jake and Wesley?"

As if summoned, both sons appeared behind their father. Wesley's smile was broad. "Sarah."

Jake smiled, too, but with some hesitation. He fumbled with keys in his hand as he nodded to me.

Yes, it was awkward. George moving to Bishop wasn't the result of a spur-of-the-moment decision. The family had to have planned this for some time. When was Jake going to tell me? And why did his father move here? I assumed he was content in northern California.

Libby bantered lightly, keeping the mood cheerful. I felt anything but.

When Libby paused to take a breath, Wesley said, "Dad, this is Jake's Sarah."

Jake's face reddened while his father gave me a closer look. "You seem smart enough. Why don't you and Jake get on with it? Get married or whatever."

"Gee, Dad. Don't be subtle about it." Jake covered his discomfort with an odd chuckle.

I smiled at the old man. He just said what he was thinking. And what I was thinking. "George, we've got some details to work through before we can…"

"Details, details. You have to look at the big picture. What details are going to matter when you're my age?"

"Good point, George."

"Dad, let's go inside and unpack your clothes." Jake herded his father inside.

Wesley reached across the fence and laid a hand on my arm. "Give him some time. He's as miserable as I've seen him since Kristin passed. I know he'll come around."

"Thanks, Wes. It's a bit more complicated than him coming around. But I'm confident we can work things out."

George called for his younger son. Wesley flashed me a thumbs-up before going inside.

Darn. What does this mean? And what now?

# Chapter Twenty-Eight

I couldn't get away fast enough. I should've seen Jake's SUV when I walked up, but I was lost in my own thoughts. I said goodbye to Libby and walked back to the bakery.

After a quick check at Layers, I decided to go home and pick up Rusty. We both needed to stretch our legs. I had to clear my mind. I'd go for a walk along the canal.

Mom was happy to see me. "I haven't spent any time with you for days. Can we schedule dinner or something together? Maybe a walk?"

"Are you free now? I'm going to take Rusty out to the canal."

"Great. Let me change my shoes and I'm ready."

As she moved through the kitchen, tall and elegant, her brown hair brushing her shoulders, the love I felt for her was overwhelming. I'd missed her when I was away in LA, and now, I appreciated the moments we had together more than ever. As I watched her grab a light jacket, it occurred to me that she was the unchangeable bastion in my life. Together with my father, they'd shown me the great possibilities of a loving relationship. Their marriage was the standard by which to judge my own. She was also my dearest confidante.

In the car, I gave Mom the story of Libby's ambush. She didn't have much to say about Libby's underhanded tactics. At the canal, I unhooked Rusty from his leash, and we headed south. I'd brought a can of chartreuse tennis balls and threw one from the back of the car. Rusty scooped it up and darted back to me, dropping the saliva-and-dirt-covered ball at my feet.

Finally, Mom said, "Maybe you should just let the police do their job and concentrate on Jake and your future. You start your new job in a few weeks. That's got to be a stressor for you too."

I shrugged. I wasn't worried about the new job. I knew it would be different than I was used to, but I wasn't afraid of that. "Right now, I want to worry about how many times Rusty can fetch the same ball."

I made my point, and she understood. She kept the conversation light. We walked for a mile at an even pace that was best described as strolling. The afternoon breeze wafted across the sagebrush bringing the fading smell of creosote brush. I loved being home. I suddenly grabbed my mother's hand and tucked her arm under mine. I loved this woman with all my heart. And it felt like time to say it. "I love you, Mom."

She patted my hand and looked me in the eye. "I love you, too, Sarah. Sensible Sarah. Maybe too sensible?"

"So it seems." I released her arm and picked up Rusty's tennis ball, now entirely brown and gray, covered with mud and dust. Rusty scampered down the road toward the canal, and we followed. When he didn't return right away, my trouble radar went off.

Something wasn't right. I hurried after him, now at

the water's edge, his tail like a rotor on a helicopter. "What is it, boy?"

The canal had angled around, resulting in a cut bank, steep but only for a few feet. Because the current was so fast, I didn't want Rusty to fall in.

When I reached him, I was relieved to see that he hadn't gotten into the water at all. He was sniffing around under the reeds. I figured his ball had dropped into them. Mom took hold of my sweatshirt to keep me on dry land as I leaned to move the rushes aside.

An arm fell into the water. Rusty barked, scaring me out of my wits. Mom yelped as if someone had pinched her. Rusty's ball caught the current and bobbed down the canal. Rusty barked again.

"Oh my god, Sarah. It's a body. Oh my god." Mom's voice degenerated into a whimper.

"Call 911. Quick, before the body comes loose and floats away."

Mom stood there with a death grip on my sweatshirt. "Mom. Let me go. Call 911."

"Oh, yes. Oh." Her panicked look alarmed me. This frightened her beyond reason. I watched her take out her phone and tap the three-digit emergency number. "I have to report a dead body."

The dispatcher asked questions, and Mom answered, gradually coming back to her senses. I called Rusty and clipped his leash on. We would wait here for the police. On second thought, I'd give Mom another job to keep her out of the way when the cops came.

"Mom, will you take Rusty back to the car? I'll meet you there." She nodded with her brows drawn. "They'll want to talk to you, too, but you can meet them there."

Her head bobbed as she agreed. I'd never seen Mom

so flustered. It was understandable. Not many people see bodies like that.

A Bishop police officer arrived within three minutes, barreling down the canal road with a rooster tail of dust behind. I flagged her down and pointed to the corpse. It occurred to me that the PD must wonder about me. Since I'd been back in my hometown in May, I'd found three bodies.

What were the odds?

# Chapter Twenty-Nine

itch Foster arrived after the fire units. One of the emergency medical technicians waded in and confirmed the person was deceased. He looped a rope around the arm to secure the body so it wouldn't work loose and drift off.

The chief arrived soon after with Jake in his car. I caught Mitch Foster's frown out of the corner of my eye.

"Jake? You're keeping illustrious company lately." I nodded to acknowledge Frank.

Jake smiled, happy to see me and, I believe, relieved. He snaked an arm around my shoulders and gave me a squeeze. "Just glad you're okay."

That made my heart jump. "How long are you down for?"

"Next week. I go back the day after Christmas."

"That's lucky for a guy who lives at the bottom of the seniority list."

His head bobbed enthusiastically. "I lucked out. The other two lieutenants wanted to work. One's going through a divorce, and the other has in-laws at the house all month."

I caught Frank's attention. "Frank. Did one of your people take a statement from Cheri at Bishop Creek Restaurant today?"

"Don't think so. Let me check the computer." He strolled to his police unit, got in, and bent over the console. He was back in a minute. "The call for service was listed, but the reporting party canceled prior to contact. Hey, Mitch."

Foster walked over to the chief with purpose. He was a busy man, and the chief was disturbing his progress.

"Did you talk to anyone at Bishop Creek Restaurant this morning about seeing the missing girl?"

Foster looked at the chief like he was an idiot. "What does the activity log say?"

Frank's jaw clenched in the face of his subordinate's rudeness.

"No? Well, there's your answer. Besides, she canceled before we got there."

Frustrated, I sighed. "She had vital information about Maddie." I couldn't imagine why she wouldn't want to help. "She said she saw Maddie last week on Tuesday, the day she disappeared. She said a bald guy in a black muscle car drove up to the pawnshop and met another guy. The bald guy handed Maddie off to the other guy. She described him as built, like big muscles. Maddie got into a car with him, a two-door, like a Mustang."

"Unless she knows where he took her, we can't do anything. This isn't helping." Foster popped a stick of chewing gum in his mouth, turned, and left.

Jake was silent, his eyes following Foster, while Frank went over to the body. "That means there are two new players in the missing case. Norman is in the wind, but he is involved, just not in the way we suspected."

I gave him her name for someone from the PD to contact later.

The coroner had arrived. Photos were taken and evidence collected. Finally, the body was recovered to the mortician's custody. Two firefighters took ropes and edged the body from the water. Frank, Jake, and I held our breaths as the attendants pulled the body out with a great sucking sound. He must have been embedded in the mud.

While the beat unit was overseeing the operation, with Foster telling him what to do, Jake, Frank, and I all looked at the body and then glanced at each other. Foster kept his attention on the body.

The corpse was a big bald guy.

# Chapter Thirty

J ake got busy then. He and Frank huddled and seemed to make a plan. They elbowed me out of the way, so I walked the mile back to my car. I felt a stab of pride that Frank was relying on Jake's expertise to conduct this investigation. It made me a bit proud.

Mom had collected herself by then. Both she and Rusty were happy to see me. I climbed in and drove us home while Mom chattered about finding a corpse. I was pulling into the driveway when Jake texted. *Meet Wes and me for dinner at Dad's?* My stomach flopped. He wanted to see me.

Mom hopped out of the SUV. "Leftovers for dinner tonight, dear. Will you be here?"

"No, as a matter of fact. I just got a dinner invitation to Jake's dad's house. What do you think of that?"

She walked back to the driver's side and grasped my hand. "I think that's good news." Then her smile dropped. "You are going, aren't you?"

"Yes."

She patted my hand before she turned away. "Good."

Dinner was at six. I brought a bottle of zinfandel with the expectation of red meat. Wes had done most of the cooking at his house, leaving Jake to barbeque. Tonight, Jake grilled kielbasa, sweet peppers, and onions. Wes' mysterious aluminum packet off to one side was revealed at dinnertime—small red potatoes seasoned with rosemary, olive oil, salt, and pepper. I'd bought one of Marie's famous apple pies, and Wes contributed ice cream for dessert.

"Pie? And ice cream? My favorite." George smacked his lips with appreciation. "That dinner was better than a restaurant, son. How about some more of that wine?"

I topped off his and emptied the bottle in his boys' glasses. With dessert finished, George leaned back, stretching. Then he stood. "Wes, let's get these dishes done and we can go for a walk. This is a very nice neighborhood, and I'd like to enjoy it."

It sounded like he and Wes were removing themselves so Jake and I could have a moment of privacy. Jake motioned to the backyard, where three lawn chairs had been arranged earlier. I looked next door and noticed the lights were out. Libby would be in class on Tuesday nights. We'd have some time alone.

I sat in the chair Jake pointed to, and he swung the other around to face me. He looked exhausted, the lines around his eyes and mouth seemed more pronounced than usual.

"You're tired." I traced his cheekbone with an index finger. "I can see how this investigation stuff can wear you out."

He gave me the lopsided grin that I'd been longing

for. It meant I was someone special in his eyes. "That's not the only thing that wears me out."

I flashed a thin-lipped smile with a little humor in it. "I know. I know."

"Wait. Before we go there, I have something to tell you." He grasped both my hands and kissed a knuckle. "I was going to surprise you, but I see that was a mistake. You should've been in on the ground floor of this decision."

"What decision?"

"Today, I was offered the police chief's job for Bishop Police."

I was breathless for a moment. I didn't know how I was going to breathe. Then I coughed. "You applied? Without telling me?"

With a rueful grin, he admitted, "Yes, and I see it was wrong. *We* should've talked about it and decided together. That's part of our confusion. We're both independent and used to doing things our own way. I wanted this to be a gift to you. For our future."

I nodded. "And your father's moved down here to be with his boys?"

"Yes. He was a part of it, for sure. I had to take him into account. He's not getting any younger, and it will be up to Wes and me to take care of him when and if that time comes. And he's not getting any easier. I hate to think of the caregiver having to endure the brunt of his temper."

"But what about your hometown of Petaluma?"

"I'll miss it, but I can visit. There are some great wineries around there. You'll love it when we go. I'd love to show you around." He reached for my hand, took it to his lips for a sweet kiss, then frowned. "I need to go back for a few days to clean up some paperwork. I wanted to wait until after Christmas, but it can't. I'll be back by Christmas Eve."

My heart thumped at the enthusiasm he'd shown for a family Christmas. "It's a small price to pay for Christmas with the family, your dad included."

"I can't wait." He placed my hand on his heart.

I held my breath. "Does this mean we have a future?"

His lopsided grin told me yes.

## Chapter Thirty-One

M y heart was lighter the next day when I went to work, even though eleven-year-old Maddie Hall was still missing. The morning dawned clear and crisp despite weather reports of an incoming storm. We'd gotten our first frost the night after Halloween, but the days continued to be mild. Now in December, locals prepared for the transition to winter. Days filled with balmy seventy-degree weather cooled to the forties and fifties during the day. Nights would stretch below freezing.

I had Jake back in my life again. We had a future.

I'd forgotten to tell him last night in all the excitement, but I'd received a letter from Inyo County giving me a firm start date of January third.

I pulled into the tiny Layers lot, noting with satisfaction that Javier and all the bakers were there. Tiffani sometimes walked to work, so I wasn't worried about her missing Volkswagen Rabbit.

Javier waited for me in the kitchen in the middle of the bustle. I heard Charlie's voice over the crowd. He was calling for a customer to pick up their order. Javier stood, shifting his weight from one foot to another, his brow tensed into a *V*.

I dispensed with the usual greetings. "What's going on, Javier?"

"It's Tiffani, Sarah. She's not at work."

"And that's unusual how?" She was often late.

"I talked to her just yesterday, and she promised she would be here on time. She swore it to me." Javier seemed distressed that Tiffani had taken her promise so lightly. "I've called and texted her phone, and she doesn't answer."

I had bookwork to do but nothing that I couldn't put off. "Do you want to go to her apartment and see if she overslept? I'll take the counter."

"Please." He grabbed a jacket from the coatrack and was out the door.

I wasn't in my Layers uniform. I had bakery office-work scheduled for today and finishing touches on the fair. The holiday event was drawing close now, a mere three days away.

Ten minutes later, Javier called, his voice frantic. "Her roommate said she left for work already. She would've been on time."

A tiny thread of fear stitched through me. What could've happened to her? "Okay. Get back to work, and I'll call the police. Thank god we don't have to wait twenty-four hours for a missing person report."

The blond officer who walked through the door stood alert, her head on a swivel in the café while waiting for my attention. I'd seen her before. She had responded to Boulangerie answering my call reporting Reginald Bateau's homicide in the autumn. She introduced herself as Brianna Langston and recalled seeing me at the murder site.

"Yes, that was an awful situation."

"Didn't you find another body, a murder victim, a few months before?" Sensitive news making the rounds was one of the drawbacks of living in a small town. We all knew each other's business.

"Yes, I found my cousin in the desert outside of Wilkerson in May." I rubbed my eyes. "Seeing her and Reginald still bothers me sometimes."

She nodded an official police acknowledgment. "Now, you called to report an employee missing?"

"Yes, Tiffani is our barista. She starts work at six thirty in the morning but hasn't shown up."

Officer Langston glanced at her watch. "It's just eight thirty now. Have you tried contacting her at home?"

Javier whooshed in through the kitchen and stood beside me. "Yes, we called and texted. I sent the manager out to knock on her door. Her roommate told him that she'd already left for work at six twenty."

"How does she get here? Car? Bike? On foot?"

Javier answered. "She usually drives. She's almost always late, so she uses her car." He looked at me. "The car is in her garage, though. I had the roommate check."

The officer got Javier's contact information and then asked, "You said she was often late. Has she been this late before?"

"Once or twice." Admitting Tiffani's bad habits to an outsider went against Javier's grain. "But she always texted to say she was on her way."

Officer Langston nodded with a veiled dropping of her eyes. I could see the missing person case slipping away. "I'll need a physical description of her."

Javier answered. "She's twenty-two years old, white,

about five feet nine and one hundred thirty or forty pounds. Light brown hair, usually in a ponytail."

Officer Langston's eyes narrowed, and she focused on me. "Except for the age, that could be you."

I nodded. "We're the same size. In fact, I just gave her a box of my clothes."

"When you talked to the roommate, did you happen to get a description of what she was wearing this morning?"

Javier was sharp. He'd considered what information the police would need to find Tiffani. "She had chinos and a red Layers polo shirt, with a blue jacket."

At his last word, my gut felt like someone punched it. "Was it a blazer or some other kind of jacket?"

Javier squinted, trying to fathom the reason for my question. "No, it was the blazer that you gave her, remember?"

"Right. Do me a favor, Javier. Go to the computer and find out her date of birth." He walked off, leaning a bit forward. He had a job to do.

Officer Langston didn't miss much either. "This blue blazer, did you wear it?"

"Every day for two months after I moved here."

"And you gave it to Tiffani this week?"

"Monday."

"You realize that you and Tiffani look alike, and both wore the blue blazer. Could it be possible that someone detained Tiffani because she was mistaken for you?"

That hit me right between the eyes like a frozen mackerel. The same idea had wafted through my brain but not yet taken shape into words.

"Why would somebody want to hassle you?" She gave me a one-eyed squint. "Have you been getting into people's business where you shouldn't, interfering?" Uh oh. My reputation had preceded me.

The front door flew open, carried too far by a gust of wind, and slammed against the wall.

Langston turned and greeted the new arrival. "Oh, hi, Sergeant."

Mitch Foster stood in the doorway, a frown across his face.

My heart sank.

# Chapter Thirty-Two

Sergeant Foster slammed the door behind him, catching the attention of the customers. I saw a lip curl and a frown among the crowd. The customers didn't like Foster any more than I did. But it didn't matter.

While Langston briefed her sergeant quietly, Javier returned with a slip of paper with Tiffani's date of birth and home address. I took it and nodded for him to help the lady at the counter while I waited for the inevitable.

When Langston returned to me, I handed her the scrap of paper. She nodded her thanks and said, "We'll get this report done and be looking for her." She made no mention of the possible mistake in the identity of the victim. "I'll be leaving, but the sergeant will finish up here." Langston turned and left without meeting my gaze. I felt like she was embarrassed about something.

Mitch Foster stood squaring his body to mine. He'd always felt so adversarial. I wondered what he was after. "This girl is a slacker. You said yourself that she was chronically late to work." He shrugged her disappearance off like it was dirty laundry. "She's probably sleeping off a bender as we speak. That's what kids are doing these days. Staying sober for a while then going on a binge that lasts for days."

"Tiffani doesn't drink." I recalled our past conversations. "She's a diabetic and can't do alcohol."

Foster's lower lip stuck out in another dismissal. "That doesn't mean she doesn't dip into the trough now and then, does it?"

"What about her physical description and the blue blazer?"

At his blank look, I almost shouted. "Surely Officer Langston told you about how she and I look alike and wore the same blazer?"

His arms folded across his chest. "I'm sure you'd like to believe you look like a twenty-two-year-old barista, but that's stretching it."

"No, Sergeant Foster. You're focusing on the wrong thing. I think it's possible that the suspect accosted or kidnapped—or waylaid, whatever you want to call it— Tiffani because she looked like me."

"And you think somebody wants your attention bad enough to kidnap you?" He glanced around to see if anyone was listening. "Puh-leese."

I'd never forgive myself if something happened to her because of me. I began a protest which he cut off with a wave. "Enough."

To my relief, he turned and left.

The customers were happy to see his backside too.

## Chapter Thirty-Three

T he rest of the morning was busy. There was enough activity to distract me from Tiffani's absence. The local merchants held a sidewalk sale downtown, and the foot traffic was well beyond expectations. Our chamber of commerce, especially Paula, was superlative at keeping shopping local. For some people, online shopping was simple, but our chamber was marketing the sensory delights of local vendors. Try on the wool sweater at Owens Valley Sports, smell the coffee and teas at The Coffee Bean, and have a grand lunch at Mack's or Bishop Creek Restaurant. A dessert treat of pain au chocolate awaited shoppers at Layers Bakery with validation of a purchase today from a downtown merchant.

Libby worked overtime, trying to keep up with the Christmas cookie and Yule log cake orders. Three of us worked the front counter and café, with Javier on my nemesis, the espresso machine, thank goodness. Rosalyn, Javier, and I were just able to keep up with orders. After the lunch rush, customer lines slowed a bit.

I was taking change from a young girl for her donut

holes when I heard a thumping sound coming from the kitchen. Then I heard Libby shout for me. I patted the darling girl's pink knit cap, said thank you, and scooted to the kitchen.

Tiffani lay on a mat at the worktable, propping herself up on an elbow. Hair in disarray, clothes rumpled, and the infamous blue blazer ripped, she was able to look up at me. "I'm here. I'm okay."

I told Charlie to call 911 for an ambulance and the police. Then to Tiffani, "Where are you hurt?"

"I'm okay. He said he got the wrong girl. He never hurt me except when I kicked him."

"You kicked him?"

She straightened a bit, sitting on a hip. "Yeah. He scared me. He kept calling me 'Sarah' and telling me to shut up when I tried to yell."

The ambulance station was a block away, so they would be here within minutes. "He called you 'Sarah'?"

She nodded. "The lot was full this morning, so I parked down the street. When I got out of my car, he threw a blanket over my head and knocked me down."

"Nobody saw you?"

"No. It was six-thirty in the morning. Not many customers on the street at that time."

"Then what happened?" I felt a little guilty pressing her for answers, but I knew my time was limited. The ambulance would take her away, and the cops would talk to her. I didn't trust anyone connected with Mitch Foster to warn me if I needed to be careful. And it sounded like I'd have to be.

"He dragged me to a shed. It smelled like motor oil, but it was empty except for two cars. It took a while to convince him, but I showed him my driver's license.

Then he figured out he'd grabbed the wrong girl. It was that guy from the pawnshop next door."

*Norman Escher.* "Then he brought you back here?"

"He's a creep." She nodded, her nose running. Libby handed her a paper towel. "He said to tell you that he would be in touch."

I had no doubt he would if I couldn't catch him first.

# Chapter Thirty-Four

Officer Langston spoke to Tiffani before the ambulance took her to be checked out at Northern Inyo Hospital. Room in the normally spacious kitchen filled quickly with two medics, two police officers, and the regular crew.

Langston cornered me after the ambulance left. "Where can we talk?"

I pointed up the stairs. "The office."

Rusty stood on his bed, giving his tail a lazy wag. While I worked, his station was on the stairs landing that opened to the office. He weighed the threat level between a friend or foe at the new person coming into his office. When Langston reached down to pet his head, he decided she was okay and dropped back on his bed.

She chuckled. "Some guard dog you have."

"Yeah, he guards his toys and treats well." I sat at the desk.

She remained standing. "I'll get to the point because I'm not sure how much interference I'm going to have."

She leaned on the desk. "I think we were right on target with our observations this morning."

"Yeah. Tiffani told me that. Did she get a chance to tell you what happened?"

Langston nodded. "She did. There are a few things that you might be able to clear up."

"I'll do my best. Ask away."

"Confirm this for me. The person in the blue blazer was the suspect's target, not Tiffani."

"I believe so. I wore that jacket for several months when I first moved back to Bishop in May. I just gave it to her on Monday."

"Any particular reason you gave it to her?"

"It suited her more than me. Since moving back to Bishop, I've grown to be more of a sweatshirt kind of girl. And she's my size, so it was an easy decision."

Langston nodded, appearing satisfied with the answers. "Next, Tiffani mentioned that the suspect moved her to a shed that had two cars parked inside. I didn't get a chance to ask her how long it took him to get there from where she was abducted. What I'm looking for is any sounds or smells that could lead us to the shed and ultimately to the suspect."

"That's easy. I know who took her and where he stashed her."

Langston's jaw dropped. "Okay. Tell me."

"Here's the thing." I had to put the brakes on this for the moment. "This morning, your sergeant as good as told me the department wasn't going to do anything about Tiffani's disappearance. That because she was a young woman, she was out partying."

Langston's shoulders sagged.

"What are you going to do when I tell you who and where? Because I believe this is all connected with

Maddie Hall's disappearance. And I'm scared to death that that little girl is in jeopardy. We don't have a clue where she is."

The officer mulled over my concerns and finally sat down. "Okay. At the moment, we have Tiffani's righteous kidnap. That's enough for a warrant if you or she can identify him."

"Yes, but if you take him into custody, you're risking missing out on something vital that might tell you where Maddie is."

"How do you figure that?"

"I'm not sure yet. But it's Norman Escher, Maddie Hall's grandfather. He lives in a back room at the pawnshop, you know." I shook my head. "I just know if you take this guy off the street, we'll be at a dead end finding Maddie. We might assume he's hiding her, acting on his own, kidnapping Maddie to protect her from the guy fished out of the canal yesterday. If there's one bad guy, there could be more."

She frowned. "Assuming is a dirty word in my line of work."

"I could be wrong, but I think this is the tip of the iceberg. We need to find out Norman Escher's role in this."

Her face scrunched up with concern. "We're already at a dead end. The searches haven't turned up anything. Search and rescue personnel and a ton of volunteers have deployed all over the easily accessible trails from Big Pine to the county boundary at Round Valley. We have teams of volunteers searching buildings at Laws Museum, walking the canal, checking abandoned buildings as best they can. Nobody has found anything, not even a scrunchie." Then the possibilities occurred to her.

"You're not thinking about acting as bait for this guy to get to you, are you?"

"I don't know. Do you have a supervisor with a brain that you can talk to? Frank just left for Hawaii, right?"

Nodding, she sighed deeply, then straightened. "Here's what I'm thinking. We have to finish the report and get a warrant for this guy's arrest. No matter his motives, he kidnapped a girl. This will all take time. My supervisor is Mitch Foster, and he's a stickler about chain of command. The detective is out with an injury. I'm not sure who will write the search warrant. I haven't done one yet. I can jump the chain and reach out to the lieutenant, but I don't know how much good that will do."

"I have a thought. I know someone who might have an idea how to do this."

## Chapter Thirty-Five

J ake's voice sounded tinny on the FaceTime app. "We're all here. I'd like a quick roll call first and an acknowledgment that this conversation is being recorded."

"I'll start, Lieutenant Van Williams, Bishop PD, here and acknowledged."

"Jake Charters, current Petaluma Police lieutenant and future Bishop PD chief, here and acknowledged."

"Brianna Langston, patrol officer, here and acknowledged."

"Sarah Murray, here and acknowledged."

Lieutenant Williams had to prompt Mitch.

"Mitch Foster, sergeant BPD, acknowledged." Foster had chosen to aim the camera on his chest, specifically his badge. I think everyone got his message, especially with his sullen tone.

When the business was handled, Langston briefed Jake and Williams on the investigation. The recap took some time as there were questions that needed to be answered.

Langston led into my concerns about finding Maddie.

Jake asked me, "How do you know they're connected?"

"Because the suspect is Norman Escher, and he is Maddie's grandfather."

"And how do you know Norman Escher is responsible?"

"Tiffani knew him, his voice anyway, from being a neighboring business owner. He's got an unusual nasal tone. He took Tiffani to the garage behind the pawnshop. The building was locked up and vacant except for Escher's two cars. I'm pretty sure he believed he had me. What I don't understand is why he wanted me."

Lieutenant Williams spoke up. "How do you know what's inside a locked garage?"

"A little creative reconnoitering." I couldn't admit that I'd trespassed twice to a group of cops.

Foster spoke up, I imagined his lip curling with distaste. "Great. We got a civilian meddling in police business, trespassing if I read her right, and making assumptions on the suspect's identity based on circumstantial evidence. Just great."

Jake spoke up. "Van, how about you start writing a search warrant for the garage based on Sarah's testimony? If we find Escher, we do a photo lineup with the victim. If she ID's him, we snag him for kidnapping and execute the warrant to find out what's in the garage. But one more thing, and it's important. We need to put someone on Escher's garage, until the judge signs the warrant. It would be best with a view to the pawnshop too."

I had to ask. "Do you think Escher has Maddie in the garage?"

Jake answered. "It's doubtful. Tiffani would've seen or heard her. She'd have told us."

Lieutenant Williams said, "We'll do the surveillance while I get someone to do the warrant, then get it signed. We'll tail Escher if he leaves. But we cannot see both premises from outside. We can view either the garage or the pawnshop. The other issue is that it's late enough today that we'll have trouble finding a judge to sign the warrant once we get it done. It may be tomorrow morning before we can set this whole thing in motion."

Langston said, "Escher should be easy enough to keep track of, especially if he lives in the back of the pawnshop."

"Do what you can. Keep me in the loop." Jake signed off, as did the rest of us.

# Chapter Thirty-Six

The next morning, Libby jumped at me as Rusty and I came in the back door. "Hey, George isn't answering his door."

"What?" Who knew George would become so important to Libby?

With an impatient sigh, she said, "I've been checking on him. He's old, you know?"

I stifled a laugh. The notion of Libby making a routine for a neighbor who's been next door for two days amused me. She was taking him under her wing. "Does he know you're checking on him?"

"No." Her face colored. "I bring him a donut every day. He likes the bear claws best. I told him it's because he sounds like a bear a lot of the time."

I laughed. "You got away with that? He seems a bit cranky to me."

"He is cranky on the outside, but inside, he's a softy." She smiled at her insight. "I like him."

"Okay, when did you last try knocking on his door?"

"This morning. I went over on a break at seven-thirty. He's usually up by then, but there was no answer."

Jake and Wesley both had a spare key to their father's place. Jake was too far away. "I'll call Wesley."

Wesley was five minutes away, at his office on the north end of town. Ten minutes later, he called back, sounding worried. "I'm in his apartment. He's not here, Sarah."

"Did he have an appointment or something he didn't tell you about?"

"I'm looking at his calendar and there's nothing for today."

"He doesn't have a car, does he?"

"No, he sold it before he moved. He's debating about getting another one but..."

"How about a taxi or Uber?"

"There isn't a taxi service here in town. And as for the transportation apps, there's no way he'd be able to navigate one. He's got a flip phone, for crying out loud." Wesley's voice rasped with concern. He'd lost his wife in May. To lose his father this soon would be challenging, even for a man with strong faith like Wesley.

"Wesley, where could he be? Does he know anyone in town? I mean, it's been decades since he lived here."

"Yeah, and he was only here for a few years before he and Mom divorced."

"Hmm. That's when you lived up in Starlite, right?"

"Mom got the house in the divorce, and we stayed here until she passed." He cleared his throat. "I don't remember anyone in Bishop he's stayed in touch with."

I sighed. Wesley was a big boy. He could figure out what he needed to do.

He did. "I'll drive around and see if I can find him."

"Okay. Stay in touch."

"I'll call Jake. He'll want to know."

"It seems like he's moving over here just in time. There's always a family crisis going on in Bishop." I tried to laugh but couldn't squeak it out.

I couldn't sit there and do nothing. I made a phone call and then went to the front counter. "Javier, I have to leave for a while. My friend is missing, and I need to help look for him. With the lunch rush approaching, I called Rosalyn in for some extra hours. She'll be here in fewer than thirty minutes."

He took change from a customer and dropped it in the register. "Go ahead and take off if you need to. I can manage until she gets here."

With a grateful smile, I called Rusty. We trotted out to our new car and Rusty hopped in the back. This car was much easier for the dog than the Camry.

# Chapter Thirty-Seven

I called to coordinate with Wesley. He sent me a picture of George taken a few days ago so I had something to show people. Wesley had already begun searching the neighborhoods on the west side of Main Street. He'd started with West Elm Street and spiraled his way out. We decided that George would most likely be on the west side of town as Wesley felt his father was most familiar with it. I would drive the market and restaurant areas, and we'd regroup and compare notes.

It didn't take long for either of us to determine George wasn't in any of those places. We drove the main connector streets all the way from North Sierra Highway to East Line Street. We avoided the reservation as Wesley was sure his father would avoid any place without side-walks. We tag-teamed streets and neighborhoods off West Line Street. I took Mumy Lane and Reata Road while he took the McLaren Lane area.

We met at Izaak Walton Park on West Line Street. We parked opposite each other so we could converse driver to driver. "Do you want me to call my Mom? And get Tom and Anna to help?"

He sat back in the seat and squinted at the mountains with the sun hovering over the snowcapped peaks. "I just had a thought. It's a long shot, but he might be going to Starlite."

"To see his old house? You sold that, didn't you?"

"Yeah. Years ago. But with the minor gaps in his memory these days, I wouldn't put it past him to go up there."

"Lead the way. I can keep going to Lake Sabrina."

We found George hiking up the road which had transitioned to Highway 168. The turn-off for Starlite was the same road that Rusty and I often took for one of our favorite hikes in the Buttermilk Mountains. George walked along the roadside, ready to turn into Starlite. Wesley was out of his car before I even got mine pulled over.

"Dad, what are you doing?"

"Going for a walk. What does it look like?" George had a long-sleeved shirt, jeans, and tennis shoes on. He wasn't carrying water or anything that made me believe his story.

"Dad, this is miles away from home, and the elevation gain is serious. It's five thousand feet. And you're not used to this."

"Give him some water." I handed him a water bottle.

George drank, water dripping down the sides of his mouth.

"Dad…" Wesley put a hand on his father's shoulder. "Why don't you get in the car, and I'll drive us by the old place."

I blew out the breath I'd been holding. "I'm glad we

found him. Who knew he'd be so interested in his old house."

Wesley fastened his father's seatbelt and smiled. "He used to call it his cabin in the mountains. Before the divorce, we'd come up here for Christmas every year. It was great to be a family for a while."

His words struck a chord in my heart. I remembered the first Christmas I missed after I married Blaine. He'd given some excuse that I cannot recall why he couldn't make the trip to Bishop. To be with my husband on our first Christmas together, I'd had to give Mom and Dad a lame excuse to not spend the holiday with them. About the third year that happened, I began to wise up. I missed my parents and had made infrequent visits during our married years. But missing Christmas was especially difficult. It made this year so much more special.

## Chapter Thirty-Eight

When I got back to my car, I let Rusty out. We had a ten-minute hike. I kept it short as I had things to do. I called Jake and told him his father was safe. We chatted over the Subaru's hands-free phone connection the whole way down to Bishop. Only God knew how a seventy-five-year-old man walked that distance, uphill. Wes had said he'd call Jake when he got their dad home and settled in.

I decided to go back to Layers. I had phone calls to make for the Christmas Fair, and with Rosalyn working, this was the perfect opportunity.

In the office, Rusty climbed onto his bed, circling to find just the right spot. He lay down content with life.

But I wasn't content. There were a lot of things going well for me—Layers, the court reporter job, Jake, and of course, my parents and family. But Maddie Hall was still missing, and someone knew where she was. She had to be scared to death. At eleven years old, being kept from your family would be horrendous, even for a brief period of time. But Maddie was missing eleven full days now.

I glanced out my window onto the alley and buildings below. I was getting angry. The police were still sitting out on the corner watching. Nothing was happening. What happened to the search warrant?

The mini blinds moved inside the pawnshop in the window that faced the alley. The cops wouldn't have seen it. Norman was inside. At this point, I was sure that I could get more cooperation from Norman myself.

I decided in less time than it takes to tell. I would talk to Escher. I grabbed my phone, slipped it on silent mode, and trotted down the stairs. I slipped out of Layers and sidled over to the pawnshop's back door, keeping out of sight of the patrol car parked across the street.

I raised my hand to knock, and the door jerked open. A rough hand grabbed my wrist and pulled me inside. The door shut firmly behind me. I heard a deadbolt slide.

Norman Escher still had my wrist clamped in his fist. "You're that nosey twit from next door. Sarah Murray? Right?"

I nodded, thinking how foolish I'd been to believe I could manage this myself. I was at his mercy. He could do anything to me, and the cops would be outside waiting for a search warrant. What a prideful fool I was. I gathered what threads of courage I could salvage and lifted my chin.

"What are you going to do now, missy?" He leaned toward me as I bent away. His grizzled, unshaven face looked slack with fatigue. He was shorter than me by a head and was bulky. He wasn't fat, merely overweight. Big enough to push me around. "What are you doing snooping in here?"

"I wasn't snooping. I was going to knock. There wasn't anything sneaky about that." I wrestled my wrist out of his grasp. "What are you so afraid of?"

He turned away from me, hiding his deflated demeanor. "Nothing." Then, "Everything."

"It's Maddie, isn't it?"

He turned, his eyes blazing. "What do you know about Maddie?"

Suddenly he seemed more vulnerable than I'd believed. He hadn't concealed his granddaughter. He was worried about her. He's trying to find her too. He was desperate enough to try to kidnap me. He'd seen me coming and going, talking to police. He must believe I knew something about finding Maddie.

I felt like I had some leverage. Knowledge. "I know Maddie has been missing for eleven days now. I know that the police, search and rescue, and volunteers have been searching for her. The school PTA has mobilized to search the area inside the city limits. The city of Bishop has reassigned all their parks and public works staff to look for her. Two groups have already checked City Park and the outlying open range area, including a local pack outfit who's provided horses and mules for anyone who will search with them." Tom and Anna had stepped up and formulated a way to safely search for the eleven-year-old. They'd mapped out areas outside the city limits for their search. Most of the land around here was open range, so the lack of fencing could enable a youngster to hike into the desert with little impediment—initially. Nature would provide its own obstacles.

He huffed, his eyes squinting with something I couldn't put my finger on.

"Yeah?" His tone held a challenge.

Fear. It was fear I saw in his eyes. I could work with this. "I came to offer my help. I know you must be beside yourself with worry."

He looked away. When his gaze finally sought mine, his eyes were red-rimmed. "I… I'm afraid for her."

I slid over to a nearby stool. "Like I said, I came to help. I'm good at figuring things out."

"I believe you are. I've watched you with the police." His stubby fingers rubbed his chin. I could see the scales in his head weighing whether to be honest or not. "They're talking to you more than to me." He glanced out the window. He had to know they were staking the place out. He rushed across the room to check through another window without moving the shades.

"What other option do you have? The police will arrest you soon. And they can't help if you don't tell them the truth."

"I do that, and I'm in prison for the rest of my life."

"Then, it's either me, or you walk away from finding Maddie."

His voice rasped just above a whisper. "Okay."

"Then you must tell me everything. Everything. Especially if you think you're going to get in trouble for it. I've got to know."

# Chapter Thirty-Nine

Norman Escher sighed, blowing out the dark shadows that he'd been living with. Now, they'd become visible to me. I'd have to live with them for now.

He settled into the desk chair but leaned toward me as if in the telling of the story, he shortened the distance between him and me, like the story wouldn't be as bad as it really was. I let it go. There would always be a distance between Norman Escher and me. He began, "I've been a gambler all my life. Even as a kid, I'd bet on how many students would bring in their homework. When the casino went in, I thought I'd died and went to heaven. But it didn't take long for me to get eighty-sixed from the joint. I used credit cards to back my bets, and when I lost, I couldn't pay." His gaze swept the small room and store area. "This isn't exactly a thriving business."

"Go on."

"I got hooked on online gambling and got into trouble there. It wasn't too long after my last bet on BetsAreUs that some guy from LA showed up. Name was Bertram. Said he was from BetsAreUs. He told me that he was here to make my gambling debt go away. All I had to do was a few simple things. He was real nice at first. Wanted me to show him around town. We went up to Mammoth, but there wasn't much to see in the summer. He called it LA in the Pines. I even took him to an old cabin my wife's family had in Merry's Meadow near Old Mammoth. You know the area?"

I nodded. "South of Old Mammoth where Mountain Meadows Resort and Snow Creek Golf Course are now, right? It's a beautiful area, but not much goes on there. Not much hiking in the summer or skiing in the winter."

"Anyway, we were getting along fine when he told me I had to do some work. A little traveling, a trip to the bank, then back home. No sweat."

It didn't sound like *no sweat* to me.

"Wrong." His face sagged even more as the story of his foolishness came out. "He'd buttered me up. I was his money mule." His spine stiffened at his gullibility. "My job was to take a bag full of cash and make deposits at two banks in Ridgecrest, one in Inyokern, then up Highway 395 to Lone Pine. Make two deposits at different banks there, then on to Bishop. There are five accounts at five different banks in Bishop. Then some in Mammoth Lakes. One in Bridgeport and one in Gardnerville, Nevada."

"Were the accounts already set up, or did you have to do it?"

Norman shook his head. "They were already set up in different names. All I did was dump money into them. He said it was a new endeavor. Something his bosses were trying to diversify their cash flow. Money launder-ing, right?"

I nodded. It sounded so easy to slip into something so wrong. "How long have you been doing it?"

"Eight months. After a while, I worked off my debt and started to make some cash. It always bothered me, but I rationalized it. Hey, I wasn't hurting anyone, not making anyone use drugs or work the streets. But finally, it got to me. I couldn't keep doing it." He rubbed his eyes.

I thought about taking a break, but it seemed more important for him to get his story out. I waited.

"When Bertram came up last Monday with the week's shipment, I told him I was done. My debt was clear. I told him I'd kept track, and it was all paid back. He said it wasn't, the debt had compounded, and I still owed plenty. He said I couldn't quit." Norman took a few deep breaths. "We argued. He threatened me. I told him, 'Go ahead. Do what you want to me.' Then he got this gleam in his eye. He told me he had to keep me alive, but he could get to others in my family, to hurt them. At first, I guessed he meant with the scandal of what I've done. But then I realized he meant something else. He'd seen Maddie's picture on the desk." Norman turned and yanked open a drawer. He pulled out a framed school photo of Madison Hall. He propped it up on the desk and continued. "She's the most important person in the world to me. Bertram must have figured that out. He knew how to get his way."

He was silent for a few moments. "He took her. I mean, they took her."

"Wait, *they*?"

# Chapter Forty

"They." Norman nodded. "He brought some gangster with him. They showed up in separate cars, both were black muscle cars, like their boss had gotten a fleet discount for mobsters. He was a short, well-muscled guy with a smile that looks like it's going to eat you. The guy with the muscles left when Bertram gave him a high sign. Maybe when he figured I wasn't going to play ball. I don't know." Norman ran his fingers through his overly long hair. "Bertram forced me into his car and drove me out East Line Street, past the canal. We parked, and he told me his muscle-bound buddy was picking up Maddie and would keep her until I saw the error of my ways."

I'd been holding my breath. "Holy moly, Norman," I breathed out.

"I know. It gets worse. When Bertram told me his buddy was going after Maddie, I exploded. It was like someone flipped a switch. I was so angry. I hit him. He hit me back. I hit him again. He reached across toward me, and I just reacted. I smashed his head on the dashboard." His eyes beseeched me not to judge him. "There was so much blood. He died."

"What did you do next?"

He shrugged. "I panicked. I got out of the car, dragged Bertram to the canal, and pushed him in. I drove the car to Mumy Lane. No one goes out there, so I figured it would look abandoned."

"What about the blood on the blanket in the Celica?"

His eyes widened. "You've really been snooping, haven't you? It was in the Challenger. I used it to move the body to the canal. I just haven't gotten rid of it yet."

"I can fill you in on some of this. The cops fished Bertram out of the canal Tuesday afternoon. I'm sure the coroner has taken fingerprints and identified him. Guys like that usually have a rap sheet."

"No doubt. I saw what I believed was a prison tattoo on his arm once."

"You haven't heard from the muscle guy?"

Norman shook his head, then slammed a fist on the desk, upending the photo of his granddaughter. "I wish I knew where he's holding her. He wouldn't have... have killed her, would he?"

"It doesn't seem logical. The whole point was to hold her until you did what you were told to do."

His eyes turned wistful. "Her mom is sick. My daughter has breast cancer and is in Reno now, having surgery. Maddie is worried sick that her mom is going to die."

"That's a tough thing for an eleven-year-old to handle."

"She's kidnapped on top of waiting to hear about her mother. It's too much, too much for a little kid to cope with." He shook his head, long curls vibrating with tension. "Would the muscles guy wait with her until he heard from Bertram?"

An ugly notion bloomed in my head. "It's already been almost two weeks. The police have his phone. He couldn't get hold of Bertram."

"Would the muscle guy contact me?"

"If he wanted to get the original job done, he would. But it's hard to tell. If he panics, he could do anything, including leaving Maddie tied up someplace." Panic? What if he did already? What if he stashed her someplace where no one could find her?

I didn't need to follow that line of thinking. He could figure out what would happen to Maddie if she was abandoned and alone.

I shivered.

## Chapter Forty-One

N orman winced. "She's out there alone." He stood suddenly, knocking the chair over. "I've got to find her. I've already looked through abandoned buildings up and down the highway."

"Was that why you were in a hurry the day of the Christmas Parade?" Putting all the pieces together, the story was finally taking shape.

"Yeah. They had the whole road blocked off. I couldn't get to the highway unless I backtracked. That would cost me too much time."

"You didn't find anything anyway, right?"

"Not a trace." He paced across the small room. "I need help. But not from the cops. They'll put me away."

"The cops…"

"No." Norman stopped, squaring with me. His voice took on authority. "No way. They're too locked into rules to find my Maddie. It will take them too long to figure this out." He rubbed his chin, then squinted at me. "*You.* You found me when they couldn't. You're the one I need."

"Norman, we need law enforcement. I can't…"

"No, you do it alone. I'll help."

"We need the resources that law enforcement has…"

"Are you backing out?" He straightened, his spine filled with indignity. "You can't spare the time to find an eleven-year-old girl who's been kidnapped?"

"Norman…"

"Shame on you. Shame." Spittle flew from his lips as he accused me. Finding Maddie was everything to him.

He was right. Whatever his terms, I had nothing so pressing as finding a missing girl. Without the cops, it would be tougher, but her life was at stake. If she had been left alone somewhere without food or water. "All right, all right. I'll help. But we need to plan this out. We can't just go flitting around the desert looking under rocks."

"Right." He sat at his desk. Pulling out a creased and wrinkled map of Inyo County, he leaned over to study it.

"Okay. We're here." He tapped a pencil lead on the dot labeled *Bishop*. "On this side is the airport. There are some storage buildings that look abandoned. I'll take that."

"What about a vacant commercial building here in town? I'm thinking like the garage next door." I grabbed my phone and started a list in the memo app. BarBQ Bill's, Boulangerie, three vacant stores in the one and two hundred blocks of Main Street alone. There were more. So many more that I knew I'd need help.

"Norman, you go check out the airport. I've got an idea to cover the vacant buildings in town. Give me your phone number."

He did.

"I'll be in touch."

Three minutes later, I walked into Layers. My helpers-to-be were nearby. I had to recruit one more. I texted Emily to meet me at the bakery as soon as she could. *Free donuts.* There was no reason I couldn't use a little bribery to find Maddie.

My army was assembled in ten minutes. Emily made it in record time, albeit with a baby on her hip. Rosalyn had been working the front counter, Tiffani was at the demon espresso machine, and Libby had just finished cleaning up.

I opened the assembly. "This is purely voluntary."

Emily sputtered a laugh. "Right. Where's my pastry?"

"You'll get it after our job is done."

Libby looked tired but spoke up. "What exactly is our job? I have a paper to work on."

"Okay. Here's the deal. Eleven-year-old Madison Hall is missing. I know that's not news to any of you, but I have proprietary information that she has been kidnapped." I paused as they each voiced their shock. "So time is crucial. I believe that the kidnapper has left her in a building somewhere in the Bishop area."

"What makes you say that?" Emily asked, rocking Hazel.

"It's a guess. The guys who took her aren't from around here. If they had to stash a young girl, it would probably be someplace visible from the highway—or a place they already knew about."

Libby nodded. "In the latter case, we're out of luck. There are a ton of hidey-holes where she could be."

"I know. But we must look for her, just the same." I looked over the four innocent faces before me. What was I doing, getting them involved? Looking for a lost eleven-year-old girl, that's what. "I need your help checking vacant buildings downtown. I'd like to get inside and check each building, but it's unlikely that we have time for that. So I want you to check windows and doors. Ask neighbors if they've seen anyone around lately, especially Maddie. I'll send you all her picture."

I touched my phone and sent Maddie's school photo. When I heard four dings, I knew everyone had received the picture. "Now, we split up the town. Don't go farther than one block on either side of Main Street. If you can get into the building without breaking a lock, please do it. I can't guarantee you won't be arrested for trespassing, so be careful what you do."

Rosalyn raised her hand. "My uncle has a cleaning business. He has keys to some of these places. Do you want me to call him?"

"Yes. If he agrees and lets us in, we can cross these places off the list of where she could be."

# Chapter Forty-Two

L ibby was to stay at Layers and coordinate by phone with us. She used a tablet to list the premises we checked. We doubled up for safety's sake. Emily and Rosalyn paired, and Tiffani came with me. We split the town into quadrants and began on the south end. They took the east side, and we took the west.

Rosalyn's voice crackled over my phone. Her uncle would let them into three buildings on their side and two on ours. The first storefront we came to had been an antiques store with an enormous picture window that allowed a view almost all the way to the back walls. A small cubicle was tucked in a corner, likely a bathroom. We casually strolled around to the rear alley. To the passerby, we would look like a pair of ladies looking for a particular store. I hoped. The door was padlocked, and one small window barred. Too high to reach on tiptoes, Tiffani and I glanced around. No ladders, nothing that would make this easy.

"We'll have to guess on this one." I got my phone out

to text Libby with the address and disposition of our search.

"Wait," Tiffani said. "Pull that trash can over here and I'll climb up. Thank God for leggings."

"That's not safe, Tiffani."

Ignoring me, she tugged a half-full garbage can across the alley to sit under the window. "Can you get the lid?"

I did as I was told, surprised at her initiative. She tucked her phone in her shirt pocket and motioned for a boost. I leaned over with my hands cupped like a stirrup. Her agility shocked me. She was up and on top of the garbage can, peering into the slightly opened window.

"Nothing." Her voice dripped with disappointment.

"How much can you see?"

"The whole room. It's a potty and sink."

I helped her down, and we carried the garbage can back to where we found it.

The next store had been a real estate office. The front windows showed vertical shades drawn closed. I expected the interior would be as empty as the last building. Tiffani and I walked around to the alley. Closed, the back door sat before us without a padlock. Tiffani turned the door handle, and it swung open. Momentarily shocked, we stood in the doorway.

A wild shadow came toward us with a groaning noise. An arm swiped at me and pushed Tiffani aside. The smell of dirty clothing and an unwashed body blew past us as we both backpedaled. Tiffani let out a squeal.

I turned and looked for a weapon. A garbage can lid would do the trick. By the time I looked back, a middle-aged drunk wobbled down the alley without a look back at us. He paused behind a dumpster, and I looked away.

"Holy moly, Tiffani. Are you okay?"

She jumped up and down with excess adrenaline. "I'm good."

"We can head back if you want."

"No." She stood still. "I'm in this, Sarah. This guy was so desperate that he kidnapped me. I may not be very smart, but I know when I should help. I'm not quitting."

"No one said you're not smart, Tiffani. I'm glad you're here."

The third building was in the block north of East Line Street. Libby texted us that Rosalyn's uncle, Tony, would be there soon to open it. Tiffani waited for him while I talked to neighbors. The bait and tackle shop next door hadn't seen anyone looking like Maddie nor anyone suspicious. The auto repair shop two doors down said the same.

Next, I met with Tiffani and Uncle Tony at a vacant restaurant one block north. Tony was a broad-chested man of an indeterminate age. Sunglasses hung from the front of his shirt as his smile revealed one gold tooth in front. He seemed happy to help.

The place had been a café serving breakfast and lunch. It had been there for as long as I could remember. Mom and Dad had eaten there but didn't seem to be fans, so we never went back as a family. I had no idea how long it had been out of business.

Uncle Tony pushed aside the dumpster blocking the back door. His keys jangled as he slipped the key in the lock and turned the handle. Tiffani and I took a step back in case a wild man should want out. Uncle Tony marched in, and we followed. In the middle of what had been the dining room, we stood all three looking over what was in front of us. Tony whispered, "The place had been unoccupied for about three years. No one comes to look at it." He shook his head like someone was missing out on a bargain.

I heard scratching behind me. Hyperalert, I whirled around in time to see a pair of mice skitter along the baseboards where the food prep area had been. I stifled a *yikes* as Tiffani squeaked behind me. "Mice. I hate mice."

I'd had enough for one day. "Thanks, Tony. Come by Layers and Rosalyn will give you a pastry on the house."

His broad smile meant he appreciated the thank you.

"Tiffani, let's head back. I'm about done in for today."

# Chapter Forty-Three

Tiffani and I met with Libby back at the bakery. Libby told me she had let Rusty out for a piddle twice while we were gone. Rosalyn and Emily came in a few minutes later. Libby counted the buildings we checked, and they amounted to a respectable dozen. At least I'd have something to tell Norman.

"Emily, take a pie for the family. You went above and beyond normal friendship today."

She put a hand on my arm and said, "I'm glad I could help. But you're right. It's time for us to knock off. Hazel needs a change, and I'm going after that pie."

Rosalyn showed her the choices and boxed up the selection, hazelnut pie. She and Hazel marched out the back door. Rosalyn followed with Tiffani. Javier had closed out the registers, Libby and I shut off lights and locked the door.

I hugged Libby with my thanks and watched her leave on her scooter. It was time for me to go home too.

But something nagged at me. I was missing something, someplace where she could be. I reached for my key fob to let Rusty in the back of the car when I felt a jolt go through me. My fingers touched the spare key I'd forgotten to return to Boulangerie. What more obvious place was there on Main Street in Bishop?

It was obviously vacant. Almost abandoned. I had to check.

# Chapter Forty-Four

I felt guilty even before I got to the legendary bakery. I had no right to go inside. Judith Bateau had made that clear months ago. But now, I wasn't even sure she owned it. The bank could have foreclosed on it for all I knew. Larry Nixon from the bank had intimated the Bateaus owed on the mortgage. Not that it mattered. No owner would welcome a snoopy neighbor prowling around inside. I turned my headlights out before pulling into the parking lot. A nearby streetlamp shone enough light to help me find a spot for my Subaru. I pulled out a flashlight from the console box and got out. I looked around. All quiet.

The door opened easily, eliminating my fear that someone had changed the locks. The door swung open with a loud—it sounded loud to me—squeal. I glanced around the lot. No one around, no close neighbors to report a trespasser. I closed the door so a passing patrol car wouldn't think anything was amiss.

Inside, the cavernous French château-style building

was empty. The Boulangerie I knew was a hive of activity, employees baking and stocking pastry delights and tourists snapping them up before the other guy could grab them. Now it was a ghostly reminder of those heady days.

I tightened my grip on my keys and heard the echo. I jumped, turning this way and that before I realized I'd made the noise. Taking a deep breath, I turned on the flashlight, covering the lamp with my fingers to allow only a little illumination. I walked the perimeter, peering into alcoves and under empty counters. Circling my way to the center, I came to the spot where I'd found Reginald Bateau dead four months before. I stopped for a moment, waiting for something to inspire me. But nothing came. The place where Reginald died was bereft of emotion. As I was.

Reginald had been an incredibly difficult person to be around, let alone work for. One day this past summer, he fired his whole staff, then hired me on an interim basis to restore the business. It worked for a while, but history repeated itself when he suffered another meltdown a month later. But this time, someone sneaked in and killed him.

I shivered as I recalled seeing his body lying on the kitchen floor, macabre icing decorations over his nose and mouth. The bread knife sticking out of his chest made the ornamentation unnecessary. Someone had a ghoulish sense of humor.

I moved on, pushing the memories aside. This kitchen is where I'd first met Javier. As a lead worker here, he'd come to Layers seeking work after Reginald's murder. I was happy to hire him. An innovative thinker, he brought cost and time-saving advancements to Layers.

I counted on him for the day-to-day running of the bakery. He'd also recruited his sister-in-law, another great employee.

The pantry was bare. With no supplies left, the place had been cleared of anything of value, except for counters, faucets, and fixtures. Even the bread-proofing racks were gone. Someone had cleaned the entire first floor. One would never know a murder had been committed here.

I gripped the handrail to go up the stairs that held administrative offices and some storage rooms. A breeze rustled the elms in the parking lot and blew up against the building. A soft thud rattled the window. I almost felt an anthropomorphic sensibility. The building felt so unhappy, as if it missed all the work that bakers had done, mixing and kneading, creating tempting smells and satisfying flavors. It was as if it hated being idle. I hoped someone would buy it soon. Judith had made it clear she had no interest in operating the family business. Reginald had left her with some serious debt. To cover it, she planned to sell Boulangerie and likely her home too. Her son, Devon, would never see the inside of a bakery again as he was rotting in prison for cold-blooded murder.

The offices were empty. Someone had the furniture and office equipment removed, the water and electricity shut off. It was dark but with enough ambient light to see that there was nothing here. No missing child, no suggestion that she'd been here. When I left, I secured the back door with a sad, bereft feeling. I wondered at it. I hadn't really been attached to Boulangerie, but something today reached out and tugged at my heart.

Too bad I couldn't afford it. No, it was probably a good thing. I'd have to go into enormous debt to get

Boulangerie started up again. Besides, I had the county job in my near future.

I gave Rusty a break and headed my Subaru south toward the pawnshop.

# Chapter Forty-Five

A faint yellow light shone through the pawnshop window. Mom had left a voicemail that she'd keep a dinner plate for me if I needed. I punched the icon for her number.

"Thanks, Mom. Don't bother. I have no idea when I'll make it home."

"Is everything okay? I mean, are you still at the bakery?" She hated to be obvious when she snooped.

"I'm fine, Mom. Just following up on a few leads on where Maddie Hall might be."

"Now you be careful…"

"I promise I won't do anything risky. Thanks for the offer of dinner. I'll pick up something later. See you soon. I love you." We disconnected.

Now, it was time for me to fill in Norman. I dreaded facing him, but he had to know.

Norman opened the door quickly under my quiet knock.

"Well?" He sat at his desk, and I dropped to a stool.

"I recruited some friends to help search. We tackled

twelve vacant buildings in the downtown corridor. There are more, but we checked off a dozen today. Nothing."

The hope in his face faded and turned to anger. He picked up a paperback book and threw it across the room. "That poor little girl. And all this is my fault.'

"I'm sorry. I really hoped to be able to tell you something positive."

"Where did you check?"

I listed all the buildings we had searched.

"How about you? You said you looked south of town. How much territory did you cover?" I considered seeing if I could get more volunteers tomorrow to search where Norman had left off.

"Ah, I made it as far as Fish Springs." He shook his head. "There were a few buildings visible from the highway, and I looked into as many as I could. I got frustrated and came back. It's like looking for a needle in a haystack."

"Is there any chance you can bargain with these guys when they contact you?"

He shook his head. "They're holding all the cards." The hopeless look in his eyes tore at my heart. "I got nothing but the cash. I can't give it back to them."

We sat silent for a moment, both of us mulling over ideas. "Norman, are you sure you won't call the cops on this guy? I mean, even if you're in jail, they could find Maddie, and she'd be safe. That must mean something."

"No. No cops. They'll just muck everything up. I don't trust them."

An engine rumbled outside. A muscle car. Norman and I stood at the same time. He grunted a stern, "keep quiet," and shoved me into a curtain-covered niche where he had cleaning supplies stashed. I rolled onto a box of paper towels, a Costco purchase, no doubt. Something jabbed my hip. I felt around and found the phone in my pocket. I pulled it out and considered calling the police. I hesitated because I wanted Norman to know he couldn't push me around.

Just as I was readying my protest at this rough treatment, I heard Norman shout, "Muscles. What're you doing here?"

Instead of 911, I pressed voice recorder on my phone and held it to the gap between the curtain and the door frame. I was going to get this conversation recorded.

It was the guy I'd dubbed "Muscles." In a voice I could only describe as a snarl, he demanded, "Who were you talking to?"

Norman's quick reply astonished me. "No one. I was singing."

# Chapter Forty-Six

**M**uscles wasted little time. "Where's the cash?"

"I'll hand it over when you tell me where my granddaughter is."

"Sure. She's in the mountains somewhere. There weren't exactly addresses."

"In the mountains? Look around, pal. There are mountains everywhere. Give me something more specific or no cash."

Muscles huffed. "I saw a sign that read, Snow Creek Golf Course. Bertram showed me where the place was. Does that help?"

"Yeah. Now I know where she is." Through the gap, I saw Norman hand over a gym bag.

Muscles sneered. "I always knew you was a weak link." He pulled out a semi-automatic pistol as Norman turned. Muscles fired.

I squelched a scream as the man turned and left.

The door was still swinging shut when I bolted from my hiding place. A quick glance told me Muscles was gone. When I reached Norman, he was still breathing. I couldn't see where his wound was, but blood covered the floor. I turned him over.

"I'm getting you help, Norman."

"Maddie's at the family cabin."

"We'll find her, Norman. You just hold on."

I tapped 911 on my phone and told the dispatcher I needed an ambulance for a gunshot victim and the police. I gave the address and put the phone down when she told me not to hang up. "Norman, help is on the way."

But there was no response.

## Chapter Forty-Seven

I never heard sirens, but I wouldn't necessarily. The police department was only two blocks away on West Line Street, and the ambulance building was across the street from them.

I moved out of the way when the cops arrived. They had to be sure the shooter was gone before the medics could enter. As luck would have it, Sergeant Mitch Foster was the first in. He pulled me aside, pushed me onto a stool, and snapped, "Stay there."

He cleared the interior and growled into his shoulder mic. The medics came in, a larger middle-aged man and a young, stout one. They moved purposefully around the body, and I looked away. I heard the older guy say, "I'm calling him deceased at six-fifteen."

I slumped off the stool, and the younger medic put a hand out to steady me. "Easy. Let's look at you."

I put a hand up. "No, I'm okay. I just need some fresh air." I was in my Layers polo and had left my sweatshirt in the office. I stood and walked outside, the early evening chill descending from a cloudless sky. I took a deep breath and realized Rusty had been alone in the office for hours. My phone. It was still on the floor next to Norman on *record*.

Foster was on his mic giving orders when he saw me. He dropped the mic and shouted, "Get back over here. You're not released yet."

His rude order grated on my last nerve. "I'm leaving, but I'll be back. I have to get my dog. And be careful what you say." I aimed my best stink eye at the sergeant. "My phone is right next to the body, and I never shut off record."

Officer Langston arrived in time to herd me back to the rear entrance of the pawnshop. A young man dressed in an Explorer uniform sat in the patrol car's passenger seat. Langston hollered at me. "Sarah. Wait. Don't go back in there. We need to do a test on you."

"What?"

She lifted an apologetic shoulder. "A gunshot residue test." She waved to the explorer, and he jumped out of the car. He handed Langston two brown paper bags and tape.

"What's this for?"

"Put your hands out." She grabbed Rusty's leash from my fingers and tossed it to the explorer. "Hang onto him, please."

"Brianna, what is this about?"

"Foster ordered a GSR test for you. The way I figure it, this will clear you of shooting Norman Escher."

"Oh, my Lord." It dawned on me that Foster thought of me as a viable suspect in Norman Escher's death. The idea that someone could believe I was responsible for the violent death of another infuriated me. He clearly hadn't played the recorded conversation back.

An evidence technician from the sheriff's office drove

up. Foster briefed the tech and went back to ordering people around. The technician introduced himself, but I didn't catch his name. I felt my temper building at Foster's exercise of power. If he could make my life difficult, he would.

The technician unbound my hands. Then he ran a sticky disk over both hands, paying special attention to the thumb, index finger, and web between. He dropped the disk into an evidence bag, labeled it, and nodded at Officer Langston. The bagged disk went into a brown paper bag, labeled, and initialed to Sergeant Foster.

Then Langston took my statement and consulted with Foster. I couldn't believe he believed I was the shooter. If he had, I'd be under arrest or at least detained. I was neither. He was just making my life difficult.

Brianna Langston repeated her opinion from earlier. "This should rule you out. According to what you told me, you only saw the gun when the shooter pulled it out. But I'll need you to write the whole incident out in your own hand. Sign and date it, too, please."

"What about my phone?"

"I'm sorry, but it's evidence now."

"Please listen to it as soon as you can. Norman Escher bargained with the shooter—a bag of cash for the information about where the kidnapper hid his granddaughter. Before he died, Norman said she was in the family cabin. The muscles guy never said she was dead."

Langston nodded solemnly, went to Foster's side, and tugged at his elbow for attention.

# Chapter Forty-Eight

I finally made it home, exhausted from the night's activities. Rusty had a romp in the backyard while I mixed up his kibble. Guilt gnawed at me for leaving him unattended in the bakery for so long. I put some sliced-up roast beef in his bowl and hoped he'd forgive me. He did, as always.

I used Mom and Dad's landline to call Wesley.

"Wesley, I need Jake's phone number."

"You don't have it?"

"It's a long story. I'll tell you later."

He gave me the number, and I called. He picked up immediately. "Are you okay?"

"Yes," I sniffed. "No thanks to Mitch Foster. What a tool."

His chair squeaked as I imagined him sitting back in it. "What did he do now."

"I'll get to that later." I gave him the briefest version of Norman's murder with as much detail as I could. I cut across his protest because I had important news to tell him. "But he's got my phone bagged up for evidence, and it's got the location where they took Maddie."

The chair squeaked as he sat up. "The bad guy gave it up?"

"Yes, but not an address. Some of those cabins in the mountains don't officially exist anymore."

"Huh?"

"Some places were built long before the Forest Service mapped the areas. They ignored private residences because they were short-listed for destruction. Every four years, new administrators put demolition lower on the list of priorities so there are many abandoned buildings."

"Do you remember where he said?"

"Yeah. Old Mammoth, maybe around Snow Creek Golf Course and Mountain Meadows Ranch. But that's a vast area. There are a half dozen campgrounds and lots of trails. I wouldn't know where to start looking."

Jake was silent.

I had an idea. "Wait a minute. Norman's last words were, 'Maddie's at the family cabin.' It seems to me he said something about his wife's family having a cabin in the mountains."

"How would a person find it?"

"Darned if I know. If it was taken under eminent domain by the Forest Service, I don't know if there would be a record. Even if it was still on the Mono County tax rolls, we don't know what name it would be under."

"Now, with Norman gone, we won't have access to that info." I heard a tapping on his desk. I'd seen him tap a pencil when he was thinking. "What about Maddie's father, Will Hall? Wouldn't he know?"

"Now you're talking. He might know the name it

would be under or where the cabin is. Do you have his number?"

"You don't? Oh yeah." I heard the smile in his voice. "You don't have a phone. Foster will have it. I'll call and have him contact Will."

"Am I in trouble for jumping the chain of command?"

In my mind's eye, I could see Jake rubbing his eyes with frustration. "You leave Foster to me."

"I'm happy to do so."

"You know, Sarah. At some point, you're going to have to let the police do their job. Go back to court reporting and walking Rusty."

"You call Foster and get him on this." Nothing like ordering the chief of police to go to work. "I'll get another phone and call you in the morning."

I couldn't help but smile as I put down the handset. Both for talking to Jake and getting the location where we hoped Maddie would be.

# Chapter Forty-Nine

Friday dawned clear and crisp as only a mountain morning can. I had plenty to do today and left Rusty home with Mom. Tomorrow was the fair. At a loss without my phone where my contacts were, I decided to drop by the police station to see if I could get it released.

It was early enough that the office staff wasn't in yet, so the dispatcher told me to wait for Officer Langston.

Brianna Langston walked from the back room into the lobby within five minutes. In her hand, she held the evidence bag with my phone. I made a happy face at her, and she smiled.

"We made our own recording of the incident. It's a surprisingly good recorder, especially for the distance of the target."

"Thank you so much. I was going to get a prepaid phone, but I need my contact list. You're a lifesaver."

"By the way, the GSR test cleared you." Her smile was knowing. She'd be good leadership material.

"I knew it would. Any word on Maddie yet?"

She shook her head with a rueful smile. I got the feeling she didn't expect to find Maddie alive.

From the car, I resisted the urge to call Jake. He got off work at two in the morning, and it was seven-thirty now. He'd still be asleep. I'd call him after ten.

Layers was a hive of activity. Libby rolled out dough for what looked like croissants. But I'd given up trying to keep track of everything that came out of this kitchen. Libby would be gone in a few weeks and was diligently recording all her recipes. Charlie had all the makings of a head baker and was working hard to earn her space when she left. Marie had blossomed and actually spoke full sentences to people. Her pies and cakes were very much in demand. Rosalyn worked the front, making up sandwiches for light lunches and serving in the café. Tiffani had recovered from her kidnapping attempt and was telling her story to anyone who'd listen between lattes.

The low hum of conversation from the front and the erratic thumping from the kitchen worktable had become music to me. I'd spent the last six months here with no previous bakery experience. Heck, I can't even bake a cheesecake. But the people here, from Libby through the ranks, stepped up to fill in what I missed. We'd made a wonderful team, and I was feeling a bit melancholy about leaving Layers to go to work for the Inyo County courts.

I'd loved my court job in LA. But I needed a bit more income to be able to move out on my own. I had a future to think of. The nonprofit was taking off. Our kitchen felt almost empty without Austin and the two other kids we'd chosen to participate in Better Off Baking. At school vacation time, they had all been temporarily released to enjoy their holidays.

I made my way upstairs and settled behind the desk.

The to-do list sat squarely in front of me where I'd left it yesterday. Before I tackled it, I decided to try texting Jake to call me when he woke up.

*Good morning, sweetheart. Call when you have some time.*

The phone rang ten seconds later. "I was just going to call you."

"We must be on the same wavelength."

"What's happening in Mono County? Have they found Maddie yet?"

"Not yet. At least no one's told me if she has been found. They were going to mobilize their mounted search and rescue team to try and cover as much ground as possible. There's a winter storm warning for that area the day after tomorrow."

"Oh no. Maddie could freeze to death if she's not found."

"They're doing all they can. Foster talked to Will Hall. He didn't know of any cabin, and his wife's still in the hospital. He's going through his family papers to see if there's a deed with a lot number or something that will help us zero in on the cabin."

I sighed, feeling frustrated that I wasn't helping more. "If I didn't have these obligations here, I'd be on horseback with the SAR team."

"Let them do their job. These folks train year-round for this."

"You're right. Besides, I have the fair tomorrow. Anna asked me to help Mark on Sunday with the team in the sleigh rides on the day before Christmas Eve. He was going to do it alone, but with the surgery, he'll need help. I said yes, of course."

"Oh, I should be there by then. I'm hoping to wrap

my project up tomorrow. It's a traffic safety grant that needs to be submitted before the end of the year."

"Great. Mark and I will be shuttling tourists around the cross-country track at Mountain Meadows. We start at noon and knock off at four."

"I'll come by. I'd love to see you in action."

*Chapter Fifty*

Getting up at oh-dark-thirty was no big deal for me. Working in the bakery, there were times I had to be in at 6:00 a.m. So, I was the first to arrive at the TriCounty Fairgrounds Charles Brown Auditorium. Also, I was the only one who had the keys. I lugged in my boxes of scavenger hunt clues and the prizes that had been donated. I commandeered a corner at the scavenger hunt table for my stuff.

I wasn't alone long. Vendors began to arrive before dawn to set up. Christmas was always a labor-intensive fair because of all the little geegaws that had to be unwrapped and set up for display. At last count, I'd had to make space for two more vendors for a total of thirty. I'd hoped for twenty-five, so the participation exceeded my expectations. Three food trucks parked outside, and two snack stands were setting up inside, including a Layers counter with coffee, hot chocolate, and Christmas cookies.

Tom and Anna had tons of fun labeling their Christmas-themed bagged treats. They'd settled on Penguin

Poop Chocolate Chips, Grinch Burger Mints, Elf Bait (really M&Ms), peanuts in shells were Reindeer Droppings, and lastly, popcorn balls became Snowballs.

I got a cup of coffee from Tiffani and walked through the room. By ten o'clock, everyone was ready to roll. Satisfied, I tucked my empty cup with my scavenger hunt things and opened the doors.

I had to run to get out of their way. I'd never experienced the rush of eager Christmas shoppers like this. During the selection period, I'd chosen Charles Brown Auditorium because it could hold up to seventeen hundred people. At a glance, I estimated there might be over a thousand at the beginning of the fair. Now I worried vendors would run out of material to sell before we closed the doors at four o'clock.

Will Hall tapped me on the shoulder. "Someone told me you are in charge."

"Why yes. I'm Sarah Murray. We've met before at the tree lighting." I didn't need to recall meeting with him at the police department that night.

His glasses magnified his haunted eyes. He'd bundled up in a suede jacket, jeans, and boots and was carrying a box. "Oh, yes." He said politely. I wasn't sure he remembered me at all. "Say, is it okay if I pass these out?" He handed me the flier with Maddie's picture on it—*Have you seen this girl?*—with the local law enforcement phone numbers.

"Of course. Were you able to come up with any information on where the cabin is?"

"How did you know?"

"I've been in touch with law enforcement over this." I tapped a flier. "Any luck?"

He shook his head like a lost puppy.

"You're looking for a family cabin, right? Did you

look at photo albums from back then? Is there a picture that can help searchers?"

"Oh, what a great idea."

I felt a bit guilty that he'd grabbed onto this tiny ray of hope. What if it didn't pan out? "Here, give me the fliers. I'll pass them out. You go home and look for clues."

"I will. But I'm supposed to pick up my wife tomorrow in Reno. She's coming home." His shoulders sagged. I wondered how he was going to tell his wife their daughter was missing. He shook his head and stumbled through the crowd and out the door.

# Chapter Fifty-One

I watched the door close behind Will Hall with a bittersweet feeling. I earnestly hoped my idea would provide a clue to Maddie's whereabouts. I was more certain than ever that the kidnapper held her in the family cabin.

So did Norman Escher with his dying breath. That ruled out an abandoned shack in the desert or somewhere on the Owens Valley floor. I was sure a cabin in the mountains was where the search parties should focus. I prayed little Maddie was still alive.

I moved through the crowd, handing out Missing Maddie fliers as well as treasure hunt clues. Children's eyes shone bright with excitement. I recalled as a child, the anticipation was as much fun as unwrapping gifts on Christmas morning and seeing cousins for a big family dinner. I saw that same expectation in their eyes. I hope that when I have kids, I make Christmas as precious as my parents had made mine.

I stopped to visit with old friends from school and rodeo days. Emily had brought her family, Matt corralling kids' sticky fingers away from vendors, then indulging them with treats. I watched them as Emily chatted beside me with an infant on her hip. "This is a fun event, Sarah. If you do this again next year, I'll be sure to have Wye Road Feeds represented."

"I'm glad you're enjoying it. Here's a flier for the treasure hunt. You'll need three for each of your kids." I handed them over, and she passed them to Matt. He looked at the paper and knelt to translate the words to kid's language. What a great dad he was.

One of the vendors, Scentsory Delights, brought scents to sell—candles, potpourris, infusion concoctions, and diffusers, both machine and sticks. The smells in the room would've been wonderful, but the addition of this vendor made it spectacular. The evocative fragrance of pine trees with a hint of Christmas cookies made fair-goers flock to the food booths and trucks as well as the tree decorating. Santa, who in everyday life was my Uncle Tom, sat in a throne-like chair beside the huge lighted tree that was in evolutions of decorations. He listened attentively to each child's secret wish and indulged them with vague but hopeful promises. Periodically, he'd crook an arthritic finger at a waiting parent who would sneak over for a conference while Missus Claus plied the child with candy canes.

The Gibsons took their holiday roles seriously, so when the opportunity came around for the Christmas Candy booth, they signed up and cajoled Mark and another cousin to staff it while they listened to children's Christmas wishes. Santa's throne was nearest to the candy booth, so Anna could keep an eye on Mark. His shoulder was mending after the surgery, but he still had limited mobility. I was delighted to see him smiling at kids and laughing with their parents. He had to know many of them.

I meandered over to the candy booth and picked up a bag of Grinch Burger Mints. I dropped the Better Off Baking donation through the hole in the top of the gift-wrapped coffee can. With a silly smirk, Mark handed over the ransomed goodies. "Are you ready for the sleigh rides tomorrow?"

"I am if you are," was my answer. "Will you be able to help with your sore shoulder?" At his shrug, I went on. "Your dad suggested we tack Ed up and put a winter sheet over it during the transport. That way, most of the heavy work is done before we get there. We just need to put on the bridle and hook the lines." The sleigh was a bright red cutter with gold detailing, open with seating for four. The driver and a passenger sat up front, with room for two or three in the back. A tack box fit snugly under the driver's seat. Tom had made sure that Ed, half the Belgian team used for the parade, would be ready.

"I'll be fine. You're doing the driving, right?"

"Yessir." It only made sense. A mending shoulder shouldn't hold lines attached to a twenty-two-hundred-pound horse. "You can do the tour guide dialogue. You're good at that kind of stuff."

"Okay. What time will you be at the house?"

Ed and the rest of the Gibson stock were wintering over in the southern pasture lease outside of town. Tom had kept Ed stalled in his backyard since the parade for convenience's sake. I'd tack the horse up—likely without Mark's help—load him into Tom's stock trailer and haul Mark and the rig with the Gibson's one-ton pickup. Tom had already taken the cutter sleigh up yesterday. One less thing for us to worry about. "The rides start at noon, so I'll be at your place around ten o'clock."

"And we do this until four?"

"Right. We knock off at four, four-fifteen at the latest. I checked, and sunset is at four forty. And there's a storm predicted tomorrow night. I don't want to pack up and load this big guy in the snow and the dark." Off-loading Ed at Tom's house wasn't a problem with the excellent lighting he had all around the back, the horse stalls, and the corral. "Your dad will pick up the sleigh next week."

A gaggle of kindergarten-aged kids diverted Mark's attention by asking what kind of candy was in the bags. Mark was the perfect salesperson to say *Penguin Poop* to a group of six-year-olds.

# Chapter Fifty-Two

I'd received texts throughout the fair. Because vendors often had crises that needed help, I kept an eye on my phone. When Libby showed up at noon, she had Cameron in tow. I handed them the stack of treasure hunt clues and the remaining Missing Maddie fliers. She was eager to help, passing off the Maddie fliers to Cameron. He shrugged, took them, and followed her like a puppy.

Ah, newlyweds, I thought. Would Jake and I ever be so visibly happy?

I checked the latest text. It was from Will Hall. *No luck so far. Nothing from police either. Feeling a bit desperate. Any more ideas?*

*What about checking Norman's place? Wouldn't he have pictures or even a deed?*

*Great idea. On my way.*

The Fair wound up at four o'clock, but a dozen patrons lingered longer. Vendors were reluctant to shoo them off in hopes of a sale. By five, most of the tables had been broken down, treasures packed up and loaded onto waiting pickup trucks. All the tree ornaments were happily carried off by their makers.

Libby and Cameron turned in the papers they had left. Cameron had handed out all but a dozen of the Missing Maddie fliers. The hall was finally emptying except for clusters of vendors chatting, comparing notes, I suspected. Paula, from the chamber of commerce, waved me down as the Lions Club volunteers swept the floor.

"Sarah, you are magic, I swear. Everyone is thrilled with their own success and at how well attended the event was. Families on a budget came because the event was free. They were able to entertain their children in a wonderfully community-oriented Bishop Christmas."

"I'm so glad…"

"And the vendors were ecstatic. They were over the moon with sales. Even better than the Fall Colors Festival you pulled together in September. And *that* was a raving success." Paula's shoulder-length curls shook with enthusiasm. I pictured the petite blond leaning over her shop display case of high-end watches, gushing over the latest feature.

"Thanks, Paula. I'm glad I could put this together. I kept notes, like I did with the Fall Colors Festival, in case you want to do it again next year."

"Great idea, Sarah. I'm sure we'll be talking to you about them both."

"I'll email you the notes for the events." My phone chimed an incoming text. "Oh, excuse me." She drifted off to chat with another volunteer.

It was Will. *I boxed up Norman's papers and albums. I must pick up my wife at eight o'clock tomorrow morning, so I'll get through what I can tonight. If I can't find anything, it*

*will be afternoon before I'll have a chance to search further.*
*Wanted you to know. Still nothing from police.*

I sighed, worrying about Maddie. Every time I saw her deep brown eyes in the poster, it tore at my heart that she was abandoned someplace, crying her eyes out, surely believing that no one cared enough to search for her.

Boy, was she wrong.

# Chapter Fifty-Three

By the time the fair ended, I was tired and hungry. As much as food had been offered there, I never found a moment when I could eat. I was looking forward to a quiet evening with Mom, Dad, and Rusty. But before I could do that, I stopped by George's apartment.

He answered my knock with a smirk and turned away, leaving the door open and the screen closed. A cowlick sticking straight up on the crown mussed his gray hair. A wrinkled flannel shirt over a white tee and baggy jeans completed the outfit. He looked like he'd slept in his clothes.

"George, I wanted to check on you. To see if you need anything."

"It's not your job to check on me," he snapped.

"Okay, then." I turned to leave.

He was back at the screen door. "Did one of the boys send you?"

"No, I…"

"Because I'm seventy-four. I'm not an invalid. I'm not sick. I don't need a babysitter."

"George, I just wanted to see if you'd had dinner yet."

"I've eaten. It may not have been a gourmet meal, but I can fend for myself."

I had no idea George harbored so much resentment and defensiveness. Jake and Wesley had both warned me he wasn't easy to get along with. But this?

"Well, sir. I can see you're just fine, so I'll leave you alone."

He stopped and mumbled. "Alone."

I waited.

"I don't much care to be alone at the moment." He shoved the screen door open, almost hitting me. This was his idea of an invitation.

I stepped inside. Jake had told me that George was living here temporarily. He'd bought a house a block away on West Elm and North Fowler Streets. A century-old one-story Craftsman-style bungalow, it needed some extensive renovations.

It came as no surprise the apartment was well-heated. George wouldn't be acclimated to the winter cold here. Jake told me that the low temperatures in winter rarely got to freezing, and highs didn't often top ninety-one in summer. His summer cabin in Starlite would have had more Bishop-like temperatures, but Jake reminded me that he never lived there full-time. It had been a summer cabin for him and the family.

I pulled off my sweatshirt and tied it around my waist. "You want some company?" I wasn't so sure I wanted to be there, but since there was every hope that George would eventually be my father-in-law, it was a small investment in time to begin a relationship.

The sparsely furnished room featured a well-broken-in recliner facing a tube-type television set and a table with two chairs in the corner going into the kitchen. No artwork, clocks, or other curios hung on the freshly painted white plaster walls. After all, he was here only temporarily.

George grumbled. "Whiskey?" He stood over a TV tray with an expensive-looking bottle of whiskey. His glass had ice in it already, as if I'd interrupted his cocktail hour.

"Oh, no thanks. How about I get myself a glass of water?" Walking into the kitchen was like stepping into a magazine layout for a 1950s room. The stove/oven combination, as well as the refrigerator, were definitely over seventy years old, although a microwave on the counter defied the date of the room. For a rental property, they were in marvelous shape.

In the cupboard sat three water glasses, four plates, and nothing else. George didn't plan to do much cooking. A napkin with the crusty remnants of a peanut butter and jelly sandwich sat on the tile counter. Dinner.

I skipped the ice. The water in the Owens Valley was pure and sweet. Local water was one of the things I missed while in LA, so I appreciated every drop. Back in the living room, I scooted a dining room chair across from his recliner, where he sat sipping his drink. "How are you finding the town? Friendly?"

He cocked his head sideways and gave a half-shrug. Not sure what to make of this, I tried another approach. "Do you get to see Wesley often?" He wouldn't get to see Jake with any regularity until he moved down here.

"Yes, I suppose." For a guy who intimated that he wanted company, he sure had a funny way of showing it.

"Jake will be here the day before Christmas Eve. Last I heard, he didn't have a moving date yet."

Finally, he squinted at me. "You know he's doing all this for you."

"What?"

"Whaddya mean, *what*? Are you ignoring all this?" He swung his arm around the duplex.

"You mean moving?"

"Yes, moving," he snapped. "I could've stayed in Novato just fine, but I wanted to be near my son."

I couldn't understand what I had done to make him angry. "Then why…"

"Because he has to be near *you*." He squinted again. With a gnarled index finger, he pushed up the glasses that had slid down his nose. "You may be prettier than Kristin, but you don't hold a candle to her spunk and drive."

Shocked into silence, I couldn't think of an appropriate retort. I guess it would be natural to compare Jake's partners, but I didn't want to engage in this debate. Best not to incur bad feelings this early in our relationship.

He plopped into the recliner, taking care not to spill his drink. "She knew my boy. She knew she couldn't make him do anything he didn't have his whole heart in." He stopped, a veil dropped over his eyes. I remembered what Jake had told me about him. He refocused on me. "That's why I gave up on the idea of him or his brother, Wes, taking over my business. The business that I built with my own two hands. I sweated over loans and bills, paid for a divorce, alimony, and the boys' child support. And I still made Charters Tax Attorney successful. It took me a while, but Kristin helped me to figure out that I couldn't force either of the boys any more than my father forced me to be a janitor. That's what he did to put me through college."

This was about him and his boys, not me.

"Kristin." His eyes grew dreamy. "Now, there was a

woman. She was bright and resourceful. She didn't need Jake for anything. A real independent woman, she was. Brought in plenty of money too. She worked for an immigration attorney. If she hadn't gotten sick, she'd be a partner by now."

No way I would measure up if he compared me to a saint. I was still alive to make mistakes.

"You aren't half the woman she was." He leaned forward, a sneer on his lips. "I'd treat him better if I was you. He's giving up his career and a beautiful home to be in Bishop with you."

"Treat him better? How am I..." I stopped myself. I didn't want to get into this with George. This was a mistake. He could have been drinking before I got there. No matter. I couldn't take his bait. I wouldn't argue with him. "George. I'm glad you're doing okay. I'll see you later."

I put down my empty glass and left.

# Chapter Fifty-Four

With the schedule for the Mountain Meadows sleigh ride, going to church Sunday morning was out of the question. I'd miss Wesley's sermon as nearly every week he preached words that stirred and motivated me. He was growing into his own as an effective, powerful preacher. His flock agreed, and the faith community was growing steadily. I was sorry to miss church. And I would've liked to take Rusty with me for the sleigh rides but decided to leave him at home. Space in the sleigh, even a roomy cutter like Tom's, could get tight fast.

On the way to Tom's to pick up Ed, I listened to a voicemail from Kelly. "Hey, just wanted you to know, a citizen called in to say he realized that he saw Madison Hall in a black car two days ago. She was looking out the back window. There was a man at the wheel driving north on Brockman Lane through the rez. The caller didn't see where the car went from there. The report is yet to be confirmed. We don't know if this is credible or not. Just thought you'd like to know." He'd left it late last night. The timestamp on the message was eleven twenty.

This might be good news. Someone seeing Maddie in a car must mean she is still alive. But now I had to concentrate on the task before me. I pulled into Tom's back driveway that led to the small pasture and pole barn to the rear of their property. Tom and Mark stood waiting for me, Mark bundled up like Ralphie in the movie, *A Christmas Story*.

The morning dawned cloudy and cold, a slight breeze blowing from the north. Tom had Ed pulled out of his corral and tied. Mark started brushing the horse with one hand, still favoring the shoulder that had been almost shattered. I took over, which is what he was aiming for, no doubt. Mark's metamorphosis from a self-centered egotist wasn't one hundred percent complete. I didn't expect miracles and was pleased with the changes he'd made in his life. That he was helpful and supportive of his parents was enough for me.

Ed would ride in the trailer with the lighter day sheet now and the winter blanket after the rides. "Keep his sheet with you after you take it off." Tom clarified the reason for two blankets as he spoke to his son. "The sheet will protect the tack from damage when Ed moves around inside the trailer. The blanket will help keep him warm after he's worked all afternoon. You never know when you might need it. Keep it with you in the cutter if you have room. Don't forget to cool him out too." Like all athletes, cooling down a horse is crucial to relax muscles, so breathing can slow and the heat generated from exercise can dissipate. That way, his body temperature can return to normal in the most natural manner. "You'll possibly be driving home in a blizzard. The weather report said heavy snow moving in later tonight with a winter storm warning. So don't drag your feet up there."

Mark nodded and tucked a neatly folded but giant-sized winter blanket into the steel box. I hung the bridles in the trailer's tack room, making sure I had a spare. Tom loaded the mild-mannered equine into the spacious trailer and tied him off. It had been years since I'd loaded a horse, so I kept my eyes open. Tom was generous with pointers. I'd have to unload Ed soon, then load him for the trip home tonight.

After Tom's few reminders about hauling a live load, we headed up the three-thousand-foot climb to the mountains. Tom's pickup was a powerful machine, and it took some getting used to after my little SUV. Mark helped with the location of the lights and windshield wipers. I should've let him drive. I'd consider wrangling him into driving home tonight. I turned on the news hoping for a weather report, but I only got the strains of Kenny Chesney and local weather. Bishop's weather was milder than Mammoth Lakes and didn't get nearly as much snow, but the white stuff was predicted to hit the valley floor late tonight. I hoped we'd get Ed hauled and put away before the storm hit.

"Thanks for helping," Mark began. "Well, actually, thanks for taking over. I'm not sure how much good I'd be with the lines." He lifted his elbow. "More mobility is what I was hoping for at this point of the recovery."

"You'll mend. You've got a great nurse." His mother, Anna, had quit her job at Layers to take care of him. She'd taken advantage of his adventure in the mountains today to finish up wrapping Christmas gifts and do some baking. With Tom in Independence for a stockman's meeting, I'm sure she was looking forward to some quiet time.

"Is that Jake guy going to be here for Christmas?" Our families had always celebrated the holidays together, one year at the Gibson's, the next at the Murray's. This year, Christmas Eve would be at Tom and Anna's, and Mom and Dad were hosting Christmas Day brunch.

"Yeah. He should be down this afternoon. He's trying to beat this snowstorm." I looked out the windshield at the burgeoning clouds. The harbingers of a storm bumped over the Sierra Nevada mountain range. I checked the temperature, and at the normal forty-three degrees, I was glad for thermal underwear under my jeans and a puffy jacket. I'd brought a new winter wool cowboy hat with a chin strap for the occasion. It should keep my head warm.

"He's a real peach, ain't he?" Mark looked out the window, not trying to hide his sarcasm.

But I couldn't let the comment go. "I like him."

"We have different perspectives." His glance toward me seemed careless, but I knew him. He was getting ready for a battle of wills. "You're around cops all the time in your job, and I'm the first one to get hollered at when something goes wrong."

"Mark, first, because I worked at the court doesn't mean I was around cops all the time. You're wrong about me. I don't have an affinity for them. They're like any other group of people, some good, some not so good." I held up a hand at his interruption. "Second, for a long time, Mark, you were the one responsible for the pranks and nonsense that went on in this town. So don't act all righteous to me."

He was silent for a few moments. I guess he figured he wasn't going to find a sympathetic shoulder to cry on. While I trusted his behavior change, I would never believe that he would become a saint.

"I still don't like him." He slouched in the seat, ignoring the beauty surrounding us as we gained elevation.

Trying to distract him from his pout, I pointed to the right, where condensation plumes from the hot springs wafted upward, triggering some fond childhood memories. "Remember that time when you, Melody, and I cut junior rodeo practice? You drove us up to the hot springs at Whitmore? Remember how hot it was? We never did go for a soak. I was too scared about being boiled alive." Fissures in the earth allow hot water from underground to reach the surface. The water from rain and snow falling on the mountains seeps deep into the earth where it is heated. Minor earthquakes shake the fractures open and release the water. The network of naturally occurring hot tubs had become both tourist and local attractions. In high school, they became locations for gatherings, often for a group soak.

All around, clusters of Jeffery and sugar pines, dressed in the lacy remnants of last week's snowfall, appeared as we approached the turnoff for Mountain Meadows Resort. Mark didn't seem to care. This sulk was a snarling reminder of the old Mark.

"You don't have to like him, Mark. You must be civil, though, so you won't embarrass the family. With all the positive inroads you've made with your mom and dad, I'd hate to see it blown to bits by rude behavior."

"Sarah, I don't like the guy. He's suspicious and small-minded. I bet he's possessive and will hold you back. I don't like it. I don't feel comfortable around him."

"Like I said, Mark…"

We had arrived. A braided young woman trotted out to the corral where I'd parked. Mark rolled down his window, beaming his flirty smile, ignoring the blast of wind.

"Hi, guys. I'm Amy. Park over there on this side of the stable. Tom Gibson dropped off the cutter inside so it will be simple to hook up." We moved, and it was easy to put horse and cutter together, indeed.

*Thank you, Tom.*

A glance at the sky made me move faster. At the end of the day, I'd be unloading Ed in a snowstorm.

# Chapter Fifty-Five

The town of Mammoth Lakes sits partially upon an 11,059-foot lava dome. In the 1930s, a Los Angeles Department of Water and Power hydrologist, Dave McCoy, noticed that Mammoth Mountain consistently held more snow than other mountains. The US Forest Service awarded him a permit to operate the ski area in 1953, and the first lift was built in 1955, thus becoming a world-class ski resort today.

To the southeast was the Mountain Meadows Resort. Mountain Meadows was new to me but had previously been an open cross-country ski track. The main building was a large log-cabin-style place, a common design in these parts. To one side was a group of small guest cabins, to the other side, a barn, modern pipe corral, and covered stall setup. The front must have been lawn during the summer but was now covered with a foot of snow from the last storm a week ago. Someone had plowed a track for us to follow for the rides.

The enthusiastic crowd waiting for us jumped and

hollered. Or maybe they jumped to keep warm. Anna had packed a half dozen green-and-red buffalo plaid woolen blankets. We broke those out to warm up the first three passengers, a young family from San Diego.

Honeymooners from New York went next, a CPA and mortgage broker. The pair giggled like children at the awe-inspiring mountains, towering trees, and striking rock formations. Mark kept up a wonderful narrative of the natural and native history of the area. His showmanship astonished me even as he talked over the jingling bells attached to Ed's surcingle, the harness that encompassed the horse's girth.

The sleigh ride was so popular that Amy had to call a halt to the lineup for the rides twenty minutes before the end of our scheduled rides. We could have run a second rig and maybe even a third to keep up with those wanting a sleigh ride.

At the end of every ride, a pair of young men from the resort herded the riders into a warming shed off the barn. Amy and another attractive young woman in braids served up hot chocolate that was kept warm on a kerosene burner. They also featured snickerdoodles and iced and decorated sugar cookies. At the end of our last ride, she offered the same to us. Mark had a gleam in his eye when he looked at Amy.

We didn't have time for this. "No thanks. We need to get going."

Mark ignored me as I pulled Ed to a post and tied his halter rope. Suddenly irritated with my less than responsible cousin, I realized my phone was vibrating. I'd turned off the ringer so as not to disturb the sleigh rides. But the call might be important.

I dug around through three layers of clothing and found my phone in my jeans pocket.

It was a text from Will Hall. *Can you call? I have news.*

The phone rang, but before he could answer, the call dropped. I texted him: *Text please, can't get through on phone*.

His answer was quick: *I found it in Norman's papers. Family cabin in the trees above Merry's Meadow, south of Snow Creek Golf on BLM land. I'm calling Mono County sheriff now.* BLM is an acronym for the Bureau of Land Management.

I called out without looking. "Mark, I need you." I couldn't believe our luck. I knew the area he described. To be so close to Maddie was unimaginable. Yet it fit with Kelly's voicemail this morning. The black car was headed north on Brockman Lane, which would've led to Highway 395 and north to Mammoth area. I hoped she was there. There was no negative to this decision. A storm was coming. Little Maddie, if she was alive, was alone in or near a cabin in the mountains. It was doubtful she even knew where she was. It had been two days since Muscles came to Bishop, so she probably hadn't eaten either.

*I'm within a half mile. I've got a horse and sleigh, will leave now. Send me best coordinates/directions possible.*

"Mark!" Darn him, he was still leaning on the counter inside the warming shed, chatting up Amy. He wasn't listening for me. Nor was he unhooking the horse, which I knew was a good thing now. But I needed his help, as limited as it might be. My phone chimed the text with the coordinates or directions of the cabin. I acknowledged and hooked up Ed's surcingle, bells jingling merrily, oblivious to the grave situation.

I scanned the parking lot but didn't see Muscle's black sedan. He was probably in the wind by now. Then a familiar white SUV drove up, and I heard Arco barking inside. *Jake.*

I yelled at my cousin. "Mark, never mind. Give me your jacket." I'd make Jake trade jackets with Mark. Jake would need the protection for where we were going.

# Chapter Fifty-Six

"**H**i, Sarah."

I threw my arms around him, happy in so many ways to see my love. "Jake, we have a job to do."

"Yeah, get to Bishop before this storm hits." His dark eyes sparkled with anticipation. "I'm looking forward to a…" There was that beautiful lopsided grin.

"Just a minute." I pulled off Jake's flatlander, not a winter-mountain-worthy jacket, and trotted over to my preoccupied cousin. I yanked off his jacket and pushed Jake's into his hands. Mark shot me a questioning look, then resumed talking to the young lady.

"What the…" I handed Jake the jacket. Mark didn't like being cold, so I was sure his jacket was rated for permafrost temperatures. As Jake shrugged into the warm jacket, I showed him the texts from Will. "How far away is this cabin?" His voice crackled with excitement, the twinkle in his eye different now, but good.

"Less than a mile as the crow flies. But the trick will be getting there before the storm." I pulled on my driving gloves, wishing they were insulated instead of leather. "While I'm getting us ready, do me a favor?"

"Sure."

"Go bust up the romance over there and commandeer all the food, water, and hot chocolate you can carry. I don't think little Maddie has eaten in two days."

Jake's borderline smirk told me he'd be delighted to interrupt Mark. Amy was helpful and stowed all the left-over cookies and pound cake in a basket. The hot chocolate thermos was empty, but she had a bucket of bottled water. She and Mark carried them to the sleigh. I got Amy's phone number and forwarded Will's directions to her. Mono County sheriff would contact her for details as I'd asked him to. When we got moving, my phone would be useful as a compass or paperweight. I hoped for the compass. I slipped it into my jacket and zipped the pocket.

"Wait." Jake grabbed my arm and looked to the clouds. "This isn't smart. This could go south fast. We should wait for search and rescue."

My gaze drilled into him. "I'm not waiting." A sliver of doubt crept into my mind. Sensible Sarah. How sensible was this?

"Sarah, think about it. We're not equipped to navigate, much less go through a storm with a horse."

The picture of Maddie sitting tied up in a corner of a drafty old cabin flashed through my mind. "I can't wait. That little girl could die."

"So could we. Then we'd be no good to anyone. They'd endanger themselves by having to come look for us." I'd heard this argument before. It was like the airline safety talk. Put the air mask on yourself before helping anyone else. His voice softened. I strained to hear over the wind. "How safe is this? The storm could grow into a blizzard. What if we get stuck out there?" He motioned to the direction where I had Ed pointed.

"That's a real possibility, Jake. But the counter to that is, what if we don't go? What if the storm lasts for two days, and Maddie hasn't had food or water in that time? She could die." I got into the sleigh and gathered up the lines. I wasn't tolerating any second thoughts. I just wanted to get on with it.

Jake glared at me. Then went to his truck and dug out sunglasses and a pair of suede gloves lined with fleece. "Well, if you're going to risk turning into a popsicle, we're coming with you. You won't be alone." He opened the truck door with his remote, and Arco shot out. He ran to a bush for a quick piddle, then to Jake with his standard adoring focus. Jake patted the seat next to me, and Arco hopped to the sleigh floor and then up, seating himself next to me. Jake got up and settled next to Arco and tugged on his gloves.

"Git on," I hollered at Ed over a gust. Bless him, the horse walked right out. He might have refused or fussed. He'd done a full day's work hauling tourists around in the snow. But he didn't balk. He must have sensed we all had a job to do today. When we get back, I'll make sure that boy gets extra carrots.

One of the older ranch hands heard of our plans and handed Jake a pair of flashlights, a kerosene lamp, and a box of matches. Then he pointed out the snow-covered fire road that would get us to Merry's Meadow. I didn't dare look at my watch. This was one of those times that not knowing was best. Already behind the clouds, the sun would drop below the Sierras soon. Then we'd be without light. Time didn't matter.

As the light grayed, the breeze picked up, blowing the misty clouds of our breath away. The cold whistled into our ears and down the back of my neck. I pointed my elbow to one of Anna's blankets. Jake picked out a green one and draped it around my shoulders. It helped. He took out another and embraced his dog and himself with a bright red one.

"How about a flashlight?" Jake offered. Not waiting for an answer, he flipped it on and illuminated the path before us. A light shower of snowflakes blew past us horizontally.

The storm had arrived.

# Chapter Fifty-Seven

I used Mammoth Mountain to my right for my bearings, then as they became obscured by clouds, the trees became my guides. The road was unmarked. Forest Service roads seldom were signed, especially in the lesser-used areas. This was rarely used. But the cabin was due south of the ranch past the golf course property.

Formed fifty thousand years ago, Mammoth was part of the Long Valley Caldera. The whole area was seismically active, often with small volcanic earthquakes, sometimes in swarms. Vents from magma beneath Mammoth Mountain emit toxic carbon dioxide gasses that accumulate in tree wells and below the snow surface. Dad had told me that the known vents are barricaded and marked as hazardous, but I kept my eye out anyway. This area looked deserted.

I handed my phone to Jake for navigation. Even without cell service, the app's compass worked. It should help to hold the correct direction. A grove of Jeffrey pines sat to one side of the trail and ponderosa pines to the other. I planned to stay between these groves. Will had directed me to turn left after the lightning-struck cedar. He said there would be a narrow trail leading to the cabin. With less than a foot of snow from last week's storm, I hoped for quick and easy going.

Sounds simple, doesn't it? It would be any other day. But today, relentless night was pressing on us with the added concern of a snowstorm. Growing up, I hadn't been in very many snowstorms like this. In school, we had snow days where we learned to ski at Mammoth Mountain Ski Area. Sometimes, a storm would blow in, and my friends and I would scurry off the mountain to a warm café and wait for the bus to take us home. I never was out in the elements for awfully long.

This was different. We had a trek ahead of us, and I sometimes felt like we were traveling blind. Gusts would blow in drifts of snow, and visibility would evaporate. Still, I kept Ed moving forward, his jingle bells deadened by the sound of the gale blowing out great clouds of moisture and condensation from his lungs. It was slow, but we made progress.

It seemed like we'd been plodding for an hour, but it couldn't have been. The darkness outlined the tree landmarks into bas-relief against the snow. Sporadically, the minimal light reflected off the snow, creating an eerie effect.

I stopped to consult my compass. We still headed in the right direction. It should be a straight shot to the meadow. I wasn't sure if we'd entered it or not.

Jake and I searched for the lightning-struck cedar using the flashlight. The snow blocked out much of the landscape and only reflected the light back.

"Look. Is that it?" He pointed to a gnarled tree trunk to the right.

"That's on the right. We need to be looking on the left side."

"You're sure?"

My teeth chattered. "No. You think we should try it?"

"Yes."

"Gee," I hollered above the storm. Ed began a ponderous turn to the right. I marveled at the obedience of this gentle giant. He had won a warm, snug place in my heart. And my heart was the only place that was warm.

We slogged up a small slope to the tree stump. Ed stopped. A juniper tree had blown over and blocked our passage. Jake hopped out, leaving the blanket behind wrapped around Arco, and trudged through the calf-deep snow. He climbed over the tree and disappeared behind it. The flashlight beam scanned the area like a laser from a Star Wars movie. He scouted around for five minutes and returned. He shook his head as he wrapped the blanket around his head and shoulders. "No cabin back there. It's a solid rock and trees."

"It was too much to hope for."

Jake hopped beside me as I whistled for Ed to gee or turn to the right.

Now we had to backtrack.

# Chapter Fifty-Eight

Finding our way back to the trail proved harder than I'd imagined. The gale had blown snow drifts over much of the meadow, obscuring our tracks. Snow piled two feet deep, and more was falling.

"I'm going to get out and walk in front with the horse. We've got to find our trail, and I have a better chance if I'm closer to the ground."

Ground? What ground? The ground was two feet below the snow surface. I scotched my snark and said, "You don't know horses. I should do it."

"You keep driving him. We have to keep moving. I'll hold on to the harness so we stay together."

"Go for the noseband. Underneath is a chin strap for a halter. You can hang on to that." He clambered down from the sleigh and tied the blanket around his shoulders. Arco snuggled close to me under my blanket. Jake's gloved hand stretched out and touched the lines. I got Ed started, and he trudged through the snow beside Jake.

A gust blew a flurry of snow and blanked out my vision. I couldn't see. Anything. I yelled. "Jake?"

A faint grunt was my answer. "Jake?" Oh, my god. Had I lost him already? "Jake?" My heart jumped to my throat. "Jake, where are you?"

Then I heard him. The beam from the flashlight went back on. "I'm here. I'm okay." Another gust blew away the snow, and I could see ahead for six feet. Ed shook his head, vibrating the lines in my fingers. The snow must be getting into his eyes. They were getting into mine. I wished I'd had goggles, even sunglasses would've helped.

Relief swept through me as I saw Jake's red blanket faintly through the snow. He'd fallen, and while getting up, he'd leaned up against Ed's flank. He collected himself and turned to pat the horse's neck. He kept a hand there to keep steady and make progress.

When Jake reached Ed's nose, he felt around for the chin strap under Ed's noseband. When he found it, I yelled, "Ready?"

He lifted his right hand in a *move-on* motion.

"Git on."

Ed stomped, then stepped forward. We plodded like that for a while. I'd lost track of any concept of time. It was dark except for the faint reflection of ambient light against the snow. I heard Jake shout, "Stop." The flashlight beam moved to our left, under Ed's head.

I turned my flashlight on to see. The beam traveled over the blizzard, one second obliterated by blowing snow and the next second clearing. It was during a clear moment that I saw our snow-covered tracks.

I yelled to Ed, "Haw." Jake had found our way.

When Ed was in the track we'd made earlier, Jake came back to the sleigh. He hoisted himself up next to me. Hunching against the frigid wind, he pulled out my phone and squinted at the compass. It pointed south. We headed to Merry's Meadow.

# Chapter Fifty-Nine

As we entered the meadow, the trees closed in on us, narrowing the trail. The forest protected us from the worst of the wind so that when we came across a giant lightning-struck cedar, it was easy to spot. The lightning had sheared off the top of the tree unevenly, leaving a grotesque twenty-foot gargoyle. A withered branch void of needles pointed to our path like an atrophied arm.

Jake nudged me with his elbow, moving Arco under his blanket. Through the blankets and layers of clothing, I barely felt it. Here was the left turn. I relied more on the lines than my voice as the wind was picking up. Snow pelted us, stinging like needles against our cheeks. After the turn, I pulled Ed up and motioned to Jake that I was going to check on the horse.

I shrugged off the blanket and dropped into the snow. It was knee-deep and getting deeper. Like Jake, I kept hold of the horse on my way to see his face. Snowflakes sat on Ed's eyelashes, and an accumulation of snow had piled around the elf hat between his ears. As I brushed them off, he shook his head as if to say, "that's not fast enough, Sarah." I wanted to check his hooves to be sure he hadn't gotten snow or ice packed, but the hoof pick sat buried under his blankets in the tack box. I wasn't sure I could pick a foot up safely anyway. I resisted brushing the snow off his rump to leave an insulating layer.

Back in the sleigh, we trudged on. A gradual elevation gain put us at about eight thousand feet above sea level. Ed was breathing just fine, but we kept the pace slow. It could have been fewer, but it felt like ten minutes later, we were able to make out the dim outline of a structure. Jake pointed it out first.

My excitement must have transmitted through the lines. I thought Ed was going to break into a trot, but he didn't. Instead, he made a hop for one stride, then dropped to his knees. I jumped out of the sleigh immediately, with Jake behind me. With a flashlight beam shining ahead, we still missed an icy obstacle. A rock?

By the time I got to Ed's head, he was standing on all fours like nothing had happened. I brushed the snow away from his knees and found two small lacerations on each. He must have found a patch of ice or iced-over rock. I scooped clean snow over his cuts. They'd already stopped bleeding. This could have been so much worse. Arco yawned from the sleigh.

Jake and I didn't need to discuss it. We stayed on foot at Ed's sides and walked toward the cabin with our equine guide. Arco looked around, not knowing what to make of this as he sat on Jake's red blanket.

The structure was set on a promontory sheltered by the Jeffrey pines surrounding it in a horseshoe shape, the front open. A rustic log cabin sat before us with a boarded-up window on each side of the boarded front door. Capped with a faded green metal roof, the cabin was dark, as dark as one would expect a vacant cabin in the wilderness. It seemed incredibly old, possibly built in the early 1900s, and *very* abandoned.

Jake walked around to me and said into my ear. "Arco and I are going to check around the building before we try to get in. Wait here." He added, "Please," when he saw my expression while shrugging off his blanket.

I wanted to come with him. Neither of us could predict what he would find. But he'd have Arco, so I nodded. Jake would have to acknowledge my experience with horses, and I'd defer to his policing skills.

He set off, his flashlight in hand like a weapon.

# Chapter Sixty

I couldn't imagine what Jake thought he might find. Muscles wouldn't have returned to free Maddie, would he? The absence of the black sedan in the ranch parking lot told me no. He'd be long gone.

Arco and Jake were back in five minutes with Jake's hand over the flashlight beam. The thinnest thread of light shone through. He spoke into my ear again and I heard him easily. "There's a back door that's locked but not boarded up. I think I can get in without too much damage."

I whispered into his ear. "Okay. I'll stay with Ed. Is there a shed on the other side? Looks like one to the right over there."

He nodded. "We'll scope it out later. I want to make entry now."

Jake waded through the snow to the sleigh's front seat and unfastened the tack box. I rooted around the box, looking for a halter rope or something to tie Ed with. Jake pocketed a hoof pick and went around to the back of the cabin, the beam of light barely visible. I pulled out a lead rope and clipped it onto Ed's chin strap, then looked around for a tree branch stout enough to tie up Ed.

A thump, a grunt, and a final bang signaled Jake had made entry. I considered all those action movie SWAT entries and smiled at Jake's. Armed with a hoof pick and flashlight, he had already done battle.

Lord, how I loved that man.

"Sarah!" Jake yelled to be heard over the storm and through the heavy log walls.

I snugged the halter rope knot on a nearby tree branch and waded through the snow around the cabin. The place sat on a rock shelf, as solid as the Bible story about the wise man who built his house on a rock. There was a firewood shed to one side, with a pounded dirt floor. The structure was not quite as big as the cabin. I made a mental note of that and walked to the back of the cabin. The door sat open, and I heard a muffled crying from inside. Arco's high-pitched canine whine accented the sobs.

*Maddie.*

I ran in to find Jake leaning over her small body, Arco circling nearby. Maddie sat in a corner, rubbing her wrists and eyeing Jake as he used his pocketknife to slice through the rope around her ankles. She sniffled and used her shoulder to wipe her nose. A fading whimper escaped her chapped lips.

"Maddie?"

She nodded, her teeth chattering and disheveled brown hair billowing around her shoulders. Arco sniffed at her face. Her tension sharp as a knife, she touched his wet nose. Her face softened.

"Maddie, we're here to help you. My name's Sarah, and this is Jake. He's a police officer."

Maddie's eyes narrowed with worry. "Is it Christmas yet? Did I miss it?"

"No, Maddie. They'll find us soon. There will be plenty of time to get home."

Her face relaxed a bit. To an eleven-year-old, what was more important than Christmas? And her mother? She wouldn't yet know her mother was coming home.

Jake steered her back on track. "Is there anyone else around here?" Arco shook the rapidly melting snow off his coat. Jake wiped the wetness from his face and said, "We'd like to find the guy who did this."

"They're gone." Her eyes dropped to her hands. "I've got to go to the bathroom."

Poor girl. How long had it been? I offered, "Oh, sure, honey. Here's my flashlight. I'll go with you and stand outside the door." Her legs were wobbly, and she needed support to walk to the bathroom. She'd been missing for over a week, and likely been tied up most of that time.

There would be time to tell her about her grandfather after we get rescued.

# Chapter Sixty-One

When personal business had been addressed, I walked to the main room with her. We sat as Jake checked out the bathroom, made five or six trips outside, and brought back the snow-filled bucket. He put it on the raised hearth to melt. When it was water, he hauled it to the back of the house. Each time, it sounded like a toilet flushing.

"I'd like to use that to give Ed some water." With a cheery nod, Jake went out once more and filled the bucket with snow to melt at the fireplace. When it sat in front of the fire, he lighted the kerosene lamp. He placed it on the kitchen table so we were able to survey the surroundings. Maddie took a seat at the kitchen table.

The cabin was a simple square divided into two small bedrooms separated by a bathroom and a living area that opened to a rudimentary kitchen. It held a three-foot butcher-block counter, a sink, and an old range with a four-burner cooktop. From the spiderwebs and dust, it was abandoned for a long time. A broken-down couch covered with a dusty Mexican serape-type blanket sat

under the front window with two equally worn upholstered chairs opposite. Jake had found Maddie tied next
to a dusty, river-rock fireplace, but it was clear someone
had been in the cabin very recently. Someone had sat in a
kitchen chair, the sink held crushed beer cans, empty
water bottles, and food wrappings. Jake flipped a light
switch. No power, what we expected. The gauge on the
propane tank sat under two feet of snow. It was more
than I wanted to deal with at the moment. At the sink,
the faucet was dry. The bathroom wouldn't work either,
then. I sighed. The pipes would've frozen if they hadn't
been insulated. It looked to me like this place hadn't
seen occupants since insulation was invented.

"Jake, I'm going to get the food and water we
brought. I'll be right back."

Maddie's face crumpled, her shoulders stiff with
alarm. Jake spoke up. "Wait, Sarah. I don't think you
should leave her right now. I'll go." He told Arco to stay
and walked out.

"Of course. How thoughtless of me." I went to
Maddie and sat at the table. "Have you been here long?"

She nodded.

"How long were you left alone?"

"This last time? Two nights."

"You haven't eaten or had anything to drink in that
time?"

She shook her head, then reached out to touch Arco's
damp fur.

Jake came in with a gust of wind and snow, carrying
the basket of food that Amy had contributed. He put it
on the counter and pulled a couple of bottled waters out
of his pockets. He opened one and handed it to her. She
drank greedily and emptied it. He opened the other and
set it on the table in front of her.

The basket had snow on it, but the moisture hadn't sogged any of the food. I unwrapped a paper plate of left-over cookies and set them in front of Maddie. She ate snickerdoodles like she hadn't had any food for two days. She hadn't. While she shoveled cookies into her mouth, I stood and went to Jake. "We're not going anywhere tonight. The storm sounds worse now than an hour ago." A gust blew against the cabin, making it sound like a freight train passing.

He glanced at the closed back door. "I think so too. We can tuck in here tonight and wait for help tomorrow or maybe haul ourselves out. Oh, here's your cell." He reached into his pants pocket and handed me the phone. I looked and saw *no service* on the screen.

"No surprise here." I took a water bottle for myself. "I agree with you. We stay. I'm going to unhook Ed from the sleigh and see if I can fit him into the woodshed."

"I'll get a bunch of that wood to keep the fire going. It's freezing in here." He saw me glance at his jeans, wet from the snow. "I'll dry out in front of the fire."

"Me too when I'm done outside." Then to Maddie, "Maddie," she'd pushed away the plate of cookies and was slurping down the rest of the water. "We aren't leaving you here alone. Jake's going to bring wood in to build a fire, and I've got to put Ed away." I decided to spare her the explanation of Ed for the moment. With a little water and food in her stomach, her face had colored a bit. At least she wasn't as pale as before.

"What day is it?"

"Two days before Christmas. The eve of Christmas Eve." She hadn't remembered.

She hung her head. "Oh yeah."

"We'll get you home before Christmas, Maddie. Don't worry." I usually tried not to make promises I couldn't guarantee, but this was different. This little girl needed something positive to hope for.

"My dad said Mom would be home by now." Tears welled up in her eyes. I wanted to comfort her, but I didn't want to get her hopes up, only to have them dashed when she got home. I knew the basics, that Maddie's mother was in the hospital, and her dad was going to pick her up today. I didn't know enough to promise Maddie her mother would be okay. Just because she was coming home didn't mean she was healing.

"When the weather breaks, Jake, Arco, and I will get you out of here."

Maddie buried her face in the crook of her arm on the table. "She's been real sick, you know."

"I'm so sorry." I put my hand on her back. "You're worried about her, aren't you?"

Her head shook as she nodded yes. What could I say to this little girl who'd already had multiple doses of adult situations to cope with? How could I console her?

Maddie lifted her head, her eyes rimmed with red, her nose dripping. "I'm afraid she'll die before I see her again. I love my mommy. I don't want her to die." Sobs racked the small body. I found myself enveloping her in my arms. I let her cry until her tears ran dry.

Chapter Sixty-Two

J ake sneaked out the door as quietly as he could. Ten minutes later, he was back with an armload of firewood. He knelt at the firebox, and arranged the wood. Keeping the fire going kept him busy while I held Maddie.

Her breathing slowed, and I thought she might have fallen asleep. But she started when I released her. Her big brown eyes were like saucers. I couldn't think of anything else to say but, "We'll take good care of you, Maddie. You can count on us."

"You bet." Jake agreed.

"Now, I need to go outside and see to Ed."

The eleven-year-olds curiosity got the better of her. "Who is Ed, and why is he outside?"

"It's a long story for later, but he's the horse who walked through the snow to find you."

Her eyes bugged out. "No. Really?"

I nodded seriously. "You like horses?" I got the faintest glimmer of a smile in return.

Her turn to nod, energetically. "Yeah. My cousin has a

horse, and she lets me pet him sometimes. I want a pony, though. They're the right size for me."

"That's a good way to start riding."

"Can I see Ed?"

"You bet, but you must wait for when this storm lets up. It's too cold outside now."

She nodded, her serious face back on. "I'll wait."

Jake stood and patted Arco's head. He whispered something in the dog's ear. Arco strolled to Maddie and sat by her chair. We closed the door behind us when we left. Maddie stood and opened the door just a crack to watch as we left. I didn't have the heart to tell her to close it. She'd been left alone enough.

Snow blew across our path. Icy lumps from the trees thudded to the ground like randomly tossed snowballs. I felt like we were in a serious game of dodgeball. I heard the crack of a branch from a tree on the far side of the cabin. It thumped to the surface with a shower of snow.

Thankfully, Ed didn't jump at the percussion. Jake helped me unhook the sleigh and slide it inside the shed on the other side of the woodpile. There was room for a half dozen cords of wood, but with only one left, we had room to store the sleigh safely. We anchored it down against wind gusts with a short scrap of rope tied to the shed. Then, assured I could handle the horse alone, he collected Anna's blankets under one arm and firewood under the other. I said to him, "You'd better get back so Maddie isn't alone too long."

"I'll go stoke the fire. You'll be okay?"

I snorted a laugh as he left and turned to Ed.

The huge horse fitted into the structure with inches to spare between the woodpile on one side and the unfinished shed wall on the other. I tied him to an open stud while I brushed the snow off and removed his tack.

I opened the tack box, pulled out his heavy blanket, and put it aside. The tack, I stowed on top of the sleigh. Then I blanketed him in his light sheet first, then the heavy one.

Just outside the front door, I picked up the dented galvanized aluminum bucket. That and a wadded-up length of rope from the shed, and I was able to make Ed as safe and comfortable as possible. I filled the bucket with snow, planning to bring it inside to melt. Ed would need water. There was nothing to feed him tonight, but I'd keep water for him.

I untied his halter rope and secured it around the surcingle, the large strap that went around his barrel to keep everything together. Then I tied an old jute rope I'd found across the shed opening onto two rusty hinges. It was a twenty-foot length. I didn't need it all, so I coiled the extra onto the hinge. If Ed pushed on the rope, it would provide little resistance that would tell him to stop. Then it would give way. Thankfully, he wasn't known for testing boundaries.

It was the best I could do for now.

# Chapter Sixty-Three

Jake had a hearty fire crackling in the fireplace when I got in. He stood directly in front of it. Maddie giggled at the steam coming off his clothes. When the bucket of snow had melted, I braved the storm again and took the water out to Ed. He looked asleep on his feet, so I put the bucket in front of his two massive hooves. I added more snow to melt and filled it to the brim. On the way back, I packed down the snow, making the path from the shed to the back door easier to traverse.

Back in the cabin, I plopped into a kitchen chair next to Maddie. She looked like a typical eleven-year-old with her hair spiked in matted snarls, and she had cookie crumbs on her chin. Her eyes held exhaustion, but that was no surprise.

"Are you okay, young lady? Can we get you anything else?"

"A Big Mac would be nice." She smiled, knowing the impossibility of her request.

"We know what to buy for your first meal when we

get out of here." Still steaming, Jake smiled across the room, Arco now at his side, his tail wagging slowly.

My feet were freezing. Snow had swamped my boots, so my socks were wet, as were my jeans from the knee down. I moved the kitchen chair to the fireplace next to Jake. I pulled off the boots and stuck my feet on the fireplace hearth. Seconds later, they were steaming too. I pulled the socks off and laid them on the hearth next to my bare feet. The heat was so intense that it almost felt like electricity shooting through. I rubbed one, then another, and got the feeling back.

When the steam off Jake stopped, he rotated himself as if he was on a barbeque spit. He faced Maddie, who sat at the kitchen table toying with a bottle cap. "Maddie. Do you mind if I ask you a couple of questions?"

A frown touched her lips, and she shrugged.

Jake offered her an out. "If you'd rather wait to talk, we can do that."

She popped the cap across the table with an index finger. "No, I can tell you what happened." She cleared her throat. "It was Tuesday. I skipped school because we were having some lame program at assembly. I'd already seen it. Dad was gone to the hospital in Reno with Mom, and Gramps was supposed to be watching me."

"Your grandfather is Norman Escher, right?"

"Yeah. He's always busy with that shop of his, so I knew I was free." She scowled at a fingernail and bit the cuticle. "I went to the dress shop, Sierra Wave. Vicki is my friend. Mom and I shop there all the time. But I didn't have enough money with me, so I didn't buy anything. When I left, I saw Gramps's friend, Bertram, at the curb."

"You knew him?"

She looked up at Jake, appearing surprised at the

question. "Sure. He's been at Gramps's store. That's where I saw him."

"Okay," Jake said. "Go on."

"He offered me a ride home. I couldn't see any reason not to get in the car. There were no *stranger danger* alarms going off in my head." She shook her wild hair at her mistake. "We went home alright. Bertram drove to the back, where the garage and yard are. There was some muscle-bound tool waiting for us in the backyard."

"Did Bertram call him by name?"

"Nah. He called him a few names I'm not allowed to repeat."

It was my turn to contribute to the story. "I called him Muscles."

Maddie nodded. "Yeah. That's the guy, Muscles. Anyway, Bertram gave him directions and drew him a map. He told Muscles that Gramps showed him this place. I guess Gramps owned it." She shrugged. "It all sounded sketchy to me, so I went for the front door. Now I was getting worried. But Bertram stopped me, and Muscles tied my hands and then put a scarf around my mouth. They bagged up food from our cabinets and my dad's beer. He's gonna be real mad when he sees they took that. We drove to Mammoth. I could tell because my ears kept popping. Oh yeah, he threw my coat over my head so I couldn't see, but I still saw a little. The mountains and trees were familiar, but I'd never been to this place before."

"This was the same day that Bertram picked you up?" Jake was taking mental notes, and the timeline was important.

She nodded, reaching for another cookie. I had a whole pound cake still in the basket. I'd save that for tomorrow morning. Surely the storm would diminish enough for SAR to find us.

She picked up her story after polishing off the cookie. "Muscles kept me here, tied up in the corner. He made a fire at night but not during the day. It's always cold in the mountains in winter." Her indignant glare would've withered Muscles had he been here. "He left every day to get food. Mostly pizza but sometimes Mickey D's. He's a real garbage gut."

Jake tried to steer her back to the topic. "He kept you here, tied up?"

Maddie nodded vigorously. "Yep. He was mean. I didn't like him one bit. He'd yell at me about things I didn't even know about. He really hollered when it snowed and he had to walk through it."

"Do you remember anything he said?"

Maddie sat and considered this. She cocked her head and began. "In sixth grade, we get videos at school about different kinds of drugs. I'm not good at remembering that stuff because I don't know anyone who uses them." She glanced at the fire and continued. "He was on something. I'd never seen a bad temper like he had. He'd cuss and yell about his so-called buddy, Bertram. Then, he'd holler about Grandpa and how he didn't do what he was told. And he yelled at me for nothing."

We waited as she studied the fire. "He hated the cops, for sure. He said so, lots of times. And…"

"…and what?" Jake prompted her.

She focused on him with a laser stare. "I don't think he would admit it, but he sounded scared. He kept me for two weeks. We'd move around, stayed in a barn one night, then here when he finally found the place. He hated hiking in here. Then, I had nothing to do but watch him when he was around. He was mad all the time. He'd leave to get food and come back. Except one time, he was gone overnight. He griped about the hike in here every time. He was really mad at somebody. Then, the last couple of days, he sounded kind of scared. I thought he might kill me." Shuddering, she looked away.

"Did he bother you?"

She squinted at his question. "Whaddya mean, besides tie me up and keep me away from my family? Yes, he bothered me."

# Chapter Sixty-Four

I fired a warning glance at Jake, who was still standing in front of the fireplace. This line of questioning could wait. Rather than put this child through the trauma again, she should rest. "I think it's about time for all of us to get some sleep. Did you have a bed to sleep in, Maddie?"

"No. I slept sitting in the corner just like you found me."

"All right. Let's check the beds and each pick one out."

Jake volunteered. "I'll sleep on the couch out here with Arco and keep the fire stoked. Looks like it's the only heat we'll get."

Maddie and I went to a bedroom and pulled back the bedspread. No sheets, no blankets. No mouse nests in the mattresses, and they looked clean enough to sleep on. I glanced around for a linen closet but didn't find one. Thank God for Anna's blankets. We wouldn't freeze tonight. With six blankets, we'd each have two.

"Okay, kids." Jake clasped his hands with relish, clearly looking forward to a bit of shut-eye. "We can talk more tomorrow. Cross your fingers that the storm abates so search and rescue can get to us in the morning." He loaded the fire with more wood and settled into the couch, Arco lying at his feet. The back rooms were cozy by now, and Jake would be warm in the living room.

Maddie balked when I pointed to a bedroom as hers. "I know I'm a big girl, but would you mind sleeping with me? I don't want to be alone."

My heart went out to her. "Of course. Now we'll have four blankets on our bed."

As exhausted as I was, I had trouble falling asleep. Was it mere hours ago that Mark and I were running sleigh rides in the meadow? It seemed like days ago.

And I worried about Ed. He had no feed tonight, nor would he tomorrow. If he had enough water, he shouldn't get colic.

Maddie fell asleep immediately. I was sure it was the best sleep she'd had all week. I couldn't say I was happy about law enforcement's response to Maddie's kidnapping. Of course, they had rules in which to operate, but it's possible they could've cost a child her life. I knew I should stay out of it, but I believed to my core that any interference I'd created helped rather than hindered the investigation.

I must have drifted off for a while. With the windows boarded up, I couldn't tell if it was still dark—or storming. The room had cooled, but the blankets kept us warm. Maddie rolled over, groaning in her sleep. I threw back the covers and padded out to the living room. The fire had dimmed to ashes with a tendril of smoke and a red glow from deep within. The wood had burned, and nothing was stacked. I glanced at the couch. Arco lay where he had been hours before.

But Jake was gone.

# Chapter Sixty-Five

I retrieved my thankfully dry boots and tugged on my vest, jacket, and parka. Jake would be outside. Probably bringing in more firewood. But I had to check. Too many things could go wrong out here. Too many things already had. I pulled my hair back into a ponytail, pushed on my hat, and set the strings close to my chin. Then I slipped on my jacket and gloves.

The wind and snow blasted me when I opened the door. There was more snow on the ground. It hardly seemed possible, but the storm had worsened. Keeping a hand on the side of the cabin, I trudged around to the woodshed, blinded until I reached the inside shelter. Ed was doing fine. His water bucket was half empty. A good sign. I refilled it with more snow and stirred until it melted.

I glanced around. I couldn't see anything outside the shed. My stomach jumped as I realized Jake wasn't here. Where else would he be? I checked behind the sleigh, but the flashlight beam swept a void.

I looked down to my feet, thinking that I could follow his tracks. There. Slight, snow-filled hollows. He'd walked to the shed and then out but had turned away from the cabin. Again, the wind blasted my face, snow crystals feeling like a hundred needles.

"Jake?" I yelled. That was pointless. My shout came back to me, unheeded.

I pulled at the jute rope I'd used to hold Ed inside. Making sure one end was tied tightly against the rusted hinge, I followed the depressions.

A mound of snow lay in front of me. I grabbed a downed tree branch and poked the pile. It gave in easily. It wasn't Jake. Another snow-covered scatter of firewood had caused the mound. Three more steps past it and I found him.

He lay near another tree branch, this one over six feet long, laying on top of a heap of snow with hints of red beneath. With a one-inch layer of white over him, I could have easily walked by. Thank goodness for the red blanket.

I dropped the rope and brushed the snow off him. "Jake, wake up." Grabbing his shoulders, I shook him. He didn't move.

I shook him again, yelling over the wind. "Jake!"

He reached for my hand and groaned. "C'mon, Jake. Get up."

I shook him harder. I hunched over close enough to see his eyes open. If he spoke, I couldn't hear it. I tugged at his arm, pulling him into a sitting position.

Knowing I couldn't carry him, I pulled his arm again. This time he made it to his feet. He shook his head and reached to me for support, still hanging onto his blanket. I slipped my arm around his waist and urged him to take a step. He was unsteady but took the step. Then another.

One length still corralled Ed. But the rope had served its purpose. I left it in the snow and followed my own faint tracks to the back door.

# Chapter Sixty-Six

I sat Jake at the fireplace, leaving him long enough to pull a club chair close by. I took off his wet jacket and moved him into the chair. He tried to speak, but nothing came out. The fire was just three meager flickers of flame, so I had to make one more trip outside.

I braced myself and did as before, touching the side of the cabin, then the shed. I packed up an armful of firewood and walked back to the cabin. I made one more trip with a huge armful of wood. After securing the door against the gale, I pulled off the fireplace screen and tossed in a pair of hefty split logs. Because the wood was sheltered, it was dry and caught quickly. Who knew how long it had been there.

Back to Jake, I made him as comfortable as I could, nestled with Anna's dry blankets. The fire blazed up soon, and I arranged Jake's red blanket on a kitchen chair to maximize drying.

I touched Jake's forehead, wondering why he wasn't awake. A tiny trickle of blood came away in my hand. Something had hit him on the head. When I felt around, my fingers touched a goose egg on his crown. I moved a kitchen chair next to him and sat.

I didn't know anything about first aid, but I'd heard that concussions were dangerous. Somewhere I'd heard that a person with a head wound isn't supposed to sleep. I shook him. "Jake, wake up. Jake."

His eyes opened.

# Chapter Sixty-Seven

"What?" He lifted his head, then his face shuddered in pain. He dropped his head onto the chair back.

"Jake, you got knocked out."

"Dang. I've got a headache." He felt around his hair and found the knot. "Ouch."

"I'm not sure if you have a concussion. I think I'm supposed to keep you awake so it doesn't get worse."

"I had my CPR and first aid refresher last year, and they said it's not necessary. You're supposed to keep checking on the person."

"I can do that." I smiled. "You want some water?" I touched his damp wavy hair.

"Yeah, that would be great."

Using Jake's pocketknife, I'd cut the narrow tops off three water bottles to make it easier to get snow inside to melt near the fireplace. I handed him one.

As he sipped, I said, "You must have gone out for firewood."

"Yep." He handed back the water and scooted up in

the chair to meet my gaze. "It was still snowing and blowing. When I walked out of the shed, the snow was so thick, I couldn't see in front of me. It all looked the same—white, like a wall. I turned to go back into the shed to get my bearings, and something hit me on the head."

"I saw a huge tree branch near you. There are lots of branches blowing around."

"That must've been it." He dropped his head against the back of the chair. Arco nosed his hand, forcing a pet. Jake smiled at his partner. "Good boy."

"I'll check on you if you want to go back to sleep." I slipped my hand over his forehead, feeling for a fever. None.

"Nah." His lopsided grin got me, just like it always did. "I have to tell you something."

"You have to tell me something? Do I have spinach between my teeth?"

He chuckled. "No. Much more important."

Feeling like he was getting ready to drop a bomb, I wanted to delay it as much as possible. "What's more important than telling me I've got spinach between my teeth?"

He dropped the corner of the blanket and reached for my hand. His was warm. "I want you to know how much I admire who and what you are."

"No spinach, huh?"

"You could've stood back and done what everyone, including me, told you to do."

I nodded as we said it simultaneously, "Let the cops manage it."

He laughed softly, and his grip tightened on my hand. "You're amazing. You knew we had to find Maddie then. It couldn't wait. You were right."

Amazed at his praise, I chewed my lip. "Is there a 'but' anywhere in that compliment?"

He tried to shake his head but stopped. It still hurt. "No. I have to say that more than ever, I trust your instincts."

"Will this be a problem when you take over as chief?"

"Undoubtedly." His lopsided grin told me that it didn't matter.

"There's something else." I cleared my throat. And chickened out. "Maybe we should wait and discuss this after we get back."

He grabbed my hand. "No. If it's important enough to bring up now, we should talk it over."

"Your dad doesn't approve of me."

Jake pulled his hand away, his eyes suddenly clear and alert. "What? Why do you think that?"

"After the Christmas Fair, I stopped by his apartment and checked on him. I've been a little concerned about his walkabout to Starlite. I just wanted to see if he was okay."

Jake was silent, visibly bracing for unwelcome news.

"He said I wasn't half the woman Kristin was." I talked over Jake's protest. "Your dad told me how wonderful she was. How she knew you so well and wouldn't make you do what wasn't in your heart. He applied it to you moving here because of me." I finally met his gaze. "He said she was the perfect partner for you."

I'd never seen Jake blush before, and it took a moment for me to realize what it was. After two seconds, he dropped his head to the back of the chair and rubbed his eyes. "I'm so sorry he said those things to you." He looked at me again. "He was right about Kristin. She was the perfect partner for me. We were happy. I loved her."

He looked away; his eyes veiled. "But there is no comparing you two. You're strong in ways she wasn't. You have the qualities that make me fall in love with you more every day. Just look at this situation. Kristin would be a nervous wreck if she was sitting where you are. But she wouldn't be here. You're the only woman, probably the only *person* in the world, who would take a horse and sleigh out in a snowstorm to rescue an eleven-year-old girl." He sat up, staring at my face. "Dad had no right to talk to you like that. I want you to know that he's wrong —dead wrong."

I could breathe again.

Jake shook his head. "I don't know if he's losing his grip on reality, has dementia, or is just a jerk. My suspicion is that he's always been a jerk, so why stop now?"

# Chapter Sixty-Eight

"What do we do now?" I heard myself ask. I was far from the helpless female, although the question sounded like I was. I had some ideas, but I wanted to hear what Jake would offer.

"We sit here until search and rescue finds us." He shrugged. "I know it's simple, but there really isn't a viable alternative. It's still snowing, and while you and I are dressed for freezing weather, Maddie isn't. She only has a sweatshirt. Hiking out now would cause more problems for her."

I chewed my lip. He was right. The trail we followed to find this place was already covered with snow. I didn't get a good enough look around to set my bearings. I wasn't even sure we could find the mountains in this whiteout blizzard.

I nodded. "I agree. But we should be listening, watching for help to arrive. I'm not saying we should station someone outside, but we're outside often enough that we should pay attention. SAR will need our help to zero in." I paused, changing gears. "That being said, we don't have much in the way of food. We have one whole pound cake, but the good news is we have water and a stack of firewood to keep warm. There isn't anything worth eating in the cupboards. This place has been abandoned too long to find food." I thought about the animals. "Arco may like some of the pound cake, and I know Ed will eat some. But there's not near enough to keep us all fueled."

With that, I stood and gathered up the three plastic bottles. I opened the door, and from the side of the path we'd made, scooped snow in each bottle, then came back in. "Sheesh, it's cold out. And still snowing, by the way." I put them on the kitchen table. The snow would melt quickly.

I stoked the fire and added another log. Jake was nodding off, and I was ready to catch a snooze. I lay on the couch, covered with a blanket, and pictured our rescue. What would it look like? Do SAR teams work in blizzards? In the dark? I suspected it depended on what kind of information they had about their targets. SAR couldn't know we found this cabin and were safe and warm, if not hungry. Would they wait until sunrise or when the snowfall quit?

What I did know was that Will Hall had found a record of this place in Norman's papers. If it was a deed, it might have GPS coordinates on it. Maybe. GPS is accurate up to six feet of the location. That was close enough.

Another scenario was that a Bureau of Land Management map might have this place on it. But it being so close to Christmas, staff might not keep offices open. I shook my head at the negatives and focused on the one positive.

Heck, I found the cabin that no one knew existed. In a snowstorm.

# Chapter Sixty-Nine

J ake and I were both dozing when Maddie got up. We awakened when she called for Arco. The dog hoisted himself up and sauntered to the bedroom. I heard her talking to him.

Jake had fallen asleep in the chair in front of the fireplace while I'd taken over the couch. The fire needed more fuel. I sat up, making plans for the morning. Jake's eyes opened with a smile that lit up that cold room. "Morning." It was a guess. With no light inside the boarded-up building, we relied on the fireplace. The kerosene in the lantern was getting low, so we used it only when it was most needed.

I smiled back, happy we'd talked about his father's disapproval of me.

Maddie walked past Jake, her fingers wrapped in the fur around Arco's neck. "Jake, what if they don't find us?" She padded over to the fireplace and sat on the hearth, Arco at her feet.

Jake sat up and looked her in the eye. "They will, Maddie. You can trust me on that."

"How do you know?"

While Jake answered her, I dressed for outside. I planned on borrowing Ed's bucket for Arco. He needed water, and I couldn't find any other container that would hold enough water for the big dog.

Maddie had more questions, including a few he couldn't answer. "We'll just have to see how that plays out, Maddie. In the meantime, Sarah and I are watching you. You're safe with us." Jake stood and stretched. He reached for his jacket and gloves. "I'm going to get more firewood." Then, over his shoulder, as he walked out the door, he said, "Maddie, bring those blankets out here, please. We can use them to keep warm."

When she ambled down the hallway to the bedroom, I opened the front door to a gray day with light snowfall. Arco had walked out with Jake and ambled off to do his business three yards away. The dog moved slowly. It appeared his joints didn't like the cold. Then, he returned to the doorstep, waiting for Jake in an obedient sit after shaking the snowflakes from his coat.

The wind still whirled between the pines, but it, too, had decreased. There was better visibility. I could make it to the shed without touching the cabin. And it was still cold.

Ed heard us coming and nickered in the hopes of a flake or two of hay. I patted his blanketed flanks. He'd lose some weight from missing two feedings, but I hoped we'd be found today sometime, and he could eat as much as he wanted when he gets back in his trailer. There were always bits of feed inside. His bucket was empty, so I loaded it up with snow.

Jake, Arco, and I came inside, Jake wrestling with an armload of firewood, and me with the bucket full of snow to melt on the hearth. It didn't take too long before

Arco had slurped half the water, dodging snow floes. He sat down beside Maddie, who had moved a club chair in front of the fire. He rooted around and found the perfect spot inside a blanket at her feet.

"I'll be right back," I said to Jake. "I want to load this up with snow and get it out to Ed."

"I'll come out with you. We could use more firewood. I want to keep the fire going as hot as possible to keep us warm. And we can hope the rescue folks will see the chimney smoke."

The wind had kicked up, but the snowfall was still light. I turned my head against the gale as I made my way to the shed, Jake following. I saw Ed shake with anticipation of a meal but couldn't hear his nicker over the wind.

The crack of a tree branch splitting from the trunk made us stop and turn to the back of the cabin. It was worse than it sounded. Under the weight of the snow, thirty feet off the top of a sugar pine snapped off and fell onto the roof. With an earsplitting groan, the cabin roof caved in.

"Maddie!" Jake shouted over the wind.

# *Chapter Seventy*

We trudged through the snow toward the cabin, the fastest pace the drifts would allow.

"Maddie, Arco!" Jake called again. We reached the door at the same time and stood, surveying the damage. The back end of the cabin collapsed under the weight of an enormous treetop burdened with snow and ice. It looked like both bedrooms and the bathroom crumpled to rubble. The front of the cabin stood, still covered by the roof, with splintered logs barely holding it up. In fact, the end of the house with the fireplace was intact. Smoke plumed merrily out the chimney like a homey Christmas card.

Jake called Maddie and Arco again, this time with Arco barking a hearty reply. Jake focused on the logs and stepped closer, reaching out to touch the wood. "If Arco's alive, there's hope for Maddie."

Encouraged, I yelled, "Maddie."

A muffled answer reached my ears. "Sarah?"

Jake took over. "Where are you, Maddie? Still by the fireplace?"

"Um, yeah."

"Is Arco nearby?"

"Yeah, he's right here with me."

"Good, Maddie. Good." Jake considered the next move. He glanced at the back door that we'd been using. Wood shards scattered for ten feet, giving an indicator of the force of the tree's impact. Logs had tumbled down, leaving only a half dozen to form the wall. The river rock that comprised the chimney and fireplace seemed to be holding up this one corner of the building. The logs were twelve inches in diameter, and I estimated ten feet long. Jake and I reached the same conclusion at the same time.

"We have to move these logs." He grimaced at the job ahead of us. "Any chance we could get Ed to help?"

I considered the tack and came up with an idea of how to attach it to a log. "I can connect and secure them to the logs. There's extra rope in the woodshed. But there's not enough room to slide the logs out without making them all fall like a house of cards. The space between the back of the house and the rock is too narrow. That might be a good tactic if this was a demolition job and not a rescue. With Maddie and Arco, any jarring motion could be catastrophic. It certainly could work on the last few logs but not the top ones."

Jake's jaw dropped. "You should've been an engineer, Sarah. Good thinking." He studied the pile of logs. "But we need these moved. What if you and I carry one at a time, and Ed can haul them out of the way? Would that work?"

"Let's get started." My stomach growled as we lifted the first log. Hunger was the least of my worries. This log weighed well over a hundred pounds. Where Jake could lift it easily, the best I could do was pushing and sliding it. We did that with four logs. Then I hooked Ed up with the jury-rigged harness. Jake tied the rope around the notch in each log and secured it to the harness and collar. Ed had done this kind of hauling for Tom before, but I hadn't. This was a new project, and I was more than a little nervous. We had to keep the horse and log on even ground. If the log rolled downhill, it could take Ed with it. For insurance, Jake looped the extra rope around the back end of the log. I drove Ed while Jake hung onto the rope and kept the log from rolling away.

It was a slow process. After two hours, we had eight logs moved, three more to go, and the rope was beginning to fray. Jake stopped to talk to Maddie. "You okay in there?"

"Yeah. Waiting."

Jake's lopsided grin told me he heard her response as a good sign.

"We're getting there. You'll be out soon."

"Okay."

"The last three are going to be difficult."

I laughed in his face. "And the first eight weren't?"

"Right." He got down on his knees, felt along the cabin wall, and pushed on a log here and there. At the bottom, he found two logs that had splintered from the foundation. God only knew what held them in place. Jake brushed the wood chips away. The three-log job now became only one.

"Wait. I'll be right back." I led Ed back to the wood-shed and tied him to the stud. I hurried back to Jake. He had something in mind.

"Sarah, listen for any creaking or sign that this wall is going to give way." Jake stretched out prone on the snow, his head at the gap in the wall. "Maddie, can you hear me?"

"Yes... yes," she moaned. "Jake, I'm getting scared. Get me out of here, please."

# Chapter Seventy-One

"We're here, sweetheart." He stuck an arm through the hole. "We'll get you out. Can you see my arm?"

She sniffled. "Uh-huh."

"Can Arco move? I want to send him out first to see if there's enough room for you without moving more logs out."

"He's here, but he's staying with me."

"He'll be with you, Maddie. He's going to lead the way."

"Okay."

Jake whistled for Arco. In seconds, the German shepherd's snout stuck out of the hole. Arco let out an anxious whine. Jake told him to come, and the dog G.I. Joe'd his way outside. Jake gave him an enthusiastic rub on his head and pushed him beside me.

"Okay now, Maddie. I want you to follow Arco. Do just what he did."

We heard her barely audible assent. A hand reached out, and Jake grabbed it. I took the other when it appeared and pulled gently. Years of accumulated volcanic dust embedded between the logs floated in the air as Maddie slid out. We all got to our feet.

"I told you we wouldn't abandon you." Jake stroked her dusty head. Maddie turned and embraced him in a fierce hug. This tough little girl had held out through impossible odds, and she felt gratitude for all Jake had done for her. My heart melted as Arco welcomed her with a nose to her cheek.

Now, on to more pragmatic matters. Jake said, "Shelter inside is out of the question. This whole structure could collapse at any minute."

"It looks seriously unstable." I debated whether to say anything. I wasn't sure he knew about this area. Then decided I must tell him. "Mammoth Lakes is a very seismically active area. There are hundreds of earthquakes every month, most too deep and too small to feel. But earthquakes aren't unusual here. One small shaker could topple this cabin."

"Well, I'd better get moving, then." Jake looked down at Maddie. "I'm glad you're wearing your sweatshirt." He glanced at me. "I'm going to try to get in there for the blankets. If we don't get rescued soon, we'll need them."

## Chapter Seventy-Two

The wind seemed calmer now than before, but snow still drifted around us in an occasional whirl of white. I looked to where the front door of the cabin had been and made my way over. If I squinted, I could see the meadow before me. The storm was clearing.

I called for Jake and Maddie. Arco came too. Jake pointed to a small stack of wood, and Arco hopped on and then sat. Maddie stared into the whiteness. Jake turned and stared toward where we'd come from yesterday. "Do you see something there?" He pointed. "It's a shadow, but it could be trees and not search and rescue."

I tried but couldn't. I couldn't see our tracks, nor could I see any help coming. "No."

"If it was search and rescue, they'd see the smoke from the chimney." We looked up. White smoke. At the risk of being negative, I asked, "How could they tell white smoke from clouds or snow flurries?"

Jake frowned and glanced out toward the meadow again and up the chimney. He turned back toward the cabin. "I wish I knew."

For some reason, I flashed back to one of Cousin Mark's more unpopular pranks. "Jake, I have an idea. Listen to this short story. Mark cut school in junior high and built a fire in the fireplace at home. Someone had told him that throwing sawdust in the fire would make the flames sparkle. It did, all right. The neighbors saw the glittering smoke coming out of the chimney and called the fire department. They said it looked like fireworks."

Jake's eyes widened. We had sawdust. We had a fire. "All we have to do is go back into the cabin with sawdust."

"I'll get the sawdust. I can go inside and do it. I'm smaller than you." I emptied Ed's bucket and scooped a bucketful of sawdust from the woodpile.

Jake took off. "I don't think so." Maddie, Arco, and I followed, all of us intent on Jake and his mission. He almost shouted he was so excited. "I'll do it." When we got to the small opening, he leaned over so Maddie couldn't hear. "I need you out here for her. And handling the horse. You're better at that than I am. This part is easy."

I loved the way he put himself in front to keep me out of danger. "Okay. Don't forget the blankets, please. We may be out here for a while before we get rescued."

Minutes later, Jake had shimmied through the small hole. He pushed five blankets through the hole and said, "Bucket." I handed it through, sawdust spilling over the sides. He disappeared again. Then his red blanket shot through the hole into my lap.

I took the blankets and draped two of them over Maddie's little shoulders. She was so little she had to bunch them up, so I tied the corners together to keep her hands free. "Let's go out front and see if the smoke sparkles like my cousin said it would."

It did. The flames set the wood dust on fire as it drifted upwards. The heat ignited new sparkles as it escaped the confines of the chimney. It was almost like watching fireworks on the Fourth of July—only cold. I thought I saw a shadow in the distance, but the flurries made me doubt myself. Nothing.

I sighed out loud and turned toward the shed, Maddie beside me. Ed had stood so quietly that Maddie didn't know he was there.

She stopped suddenly and held her breath. I waited. When she could speak, she said, "Is this Ed?"

"Yes."

She looked at me, her eyes huge with shock. "He's a horse. He's a horse."

"Yes, he is."

"Can I ride him?"

"Not now. We've got other things to do first."

She touched him, three fingers trailed along his flank. She walked up to his head and reached out to his mane. The hair here was coarser and much longer. She wrapped a lock around her index finger and stretched her other hand around his chest. Then she leaned against him in a tiny hug. I knew how she felt and couldn't cut it short.

After ten minutes, I trotted back to the opening in the cabin wall. I knelt and yelled to Jake. "If you want more, hand me the bucket."

"Have you seen anything? Heard anything?"

"Nothing yet."

Behind me, Maddie screamed. "I see them! They're coming!"

# Chapter Seventy-Three

Maddie's shout made Ed jump. It was a small movement, but given his size, I was worried that he'd knock Maddie over.

I shouldn't have been concerned. She was out of range, standing at the shed opening. The doubled-up blankets draped like a shawl as she ran the distance from the shed to the cabin. Skidding across the icy path like a major league ball player, she looked like she was stealing home. She slid to a stop near the hole, all the while shouting at Jake. "Jake, they're here." Then up at me, her face broke into the sweetest smile. "We're going home."

I tramped out front again, peering into the snow flurries. Nothing. Either her eyesight was better than mine, or she was indulging in some wishful thinking.

Then she was beside me. I curled my arm around her shoulders. "Maddie, I don't see anything."

She pointed in earnest. "There. Follow my finger."

I still couldn't see anything. Was there a smudge in the distance? But like Jake said, it could be trees or a rock. "Okay. Will you keep an eye on it? I'm going to talk to Jake."

Back at the cabin, I squatted down to speak into the hole. "Jake, there might be something there, but I don't see it. You might want to save the sawdust for when we can really see them."

"Be right out." He tossed the empty bucket and three modified water bottles out and then followed.

Even through my gloves, his back was warm when I helped him up. "Nice and warm in there?"

He chuckled as he brushed off snow and sawdust from his jacket. "Yeah, if I stay on the hearth. It gets cold anywhere else. The roof is wide open in the bedrooms. It was actually kind of breezy in there. I left the pile of sawdust at a protected spot near the fire."

I picked up the bucket. "I'll get some snow melted for Ed."

"Where's Maddie? I'll go wait with her."

"Out front." If it hadn't been half-frozen, my heart would've loved the compassion he showed for the little girl.

Even after ten minutes of stirring with a tree branch, the snow was merely a bucket of slush. I put it on the ground near Ed, and he dipped his nose into it. I stood next to him, patting his flank and ruffling his mane. He was a good boy, a tremendously patient horse. We were lucky to have him through this mess. I remembered the mare I rode through high school and what a flighty ride she could be when she was in season. She would've been a disaster in this situation.

Jake's voice cut through my reflections. "Sarah! I see them. They're coming."

I stepped outside the shed to see. Maddie ran to my side, eager to show me. "See. See?" She pointed in the same direction as before, but visibility was better now. Clouds still hung over the meadow, but they were lifting. It was clearing. The snowfall consisted of drifts blown off nearby tree branches.

She was right. I could see someone coming. It looked like a red box on tracks. A snowcat. I'd seen them in ads for Mammoth Mountain but never close-up. The low hum of an engine reached us. Maddie and I looked at each other with big grins. Then she wrapped her arms around my waist.

"Hey, hey!" Jake shouted. "You're going the wrong way." He stood in front of the cabin waving his arms. Maddie and I ran to him, the three of us watching the snowcat veer off to one side. If it kept on that path, it would miss us.

"I'm going back in. I'm going to feed sawdust into that fireplace and make a sparkler that they'll see in Bishop." He ran around to the back.

"Be careful." I guess I shouldn't worry if he set the cabin on fire as long as he wasn't inside. It was already a total loss. "Be careful, Jake."

# Chapter Seventy-Four

I had a thought. It was mildly crazy. Okay, wildly crazy, but a radical action was necessary. The snowcat was heading away from us. Jake's fireplace sparklers might help, but we needed something else—something mobile. I leaned into the hole. "Jake, I'll be back. Maddie and I are going for a walk."

The fire crackled inside. He'd built it up to quite the blaze. I heard a muffled response but couldn't make out the words. It was probably best that I didn't.

In the woodshed, Ed had finished most of the water. I dumped the rest and scooped up more sawdust for Jake. I took it back to the cabin hole and shoved it through, hollering at Jake. "Incoming." I didn't wait for a reply.

Back in the shed, I called for Maddie and pulled Ed's blanket off. Over my shoulder, I asked, "Are they still off course?"

"Yes, and they're going to miss us." Her voice was thin with panic.

I leaned down toward her so she could hear clearly.

"Okay. We're not going to let that happen. Grab Jake's red blanket and pull it around you. Tie it off like a shawl. Now, have you ever ridden a horse?"

"Oh, I've always wanted to but..." Her eyes bugged out. "You mean like Ed? No, I've only been on the pony rides at the fair."

"Okay. This will be easy. Just do what I tell you, and we'll get the rescuers' attention. We'll be out of here soon. But I need your help." I didn't really. I couldn't leave her alone. With Jake in the cabin, he couldn't keep an eye on her. She was just precocious enough not to be trustworthy alone. She had to come with me.

And I had to go.

I pulled off Ed's halter and slipped his bridle on. While not made for riding, I'd still have control. I hoped his blinders helped. Slipping the lines over my arm, I told Maddie to climb onto the woodpile. She was nervous because Ed was so big, so I had her remove the red blanket. It was easier for her to slide onto Ed's back without the cumbersome blanket. I folded it in half and handed it back to her. Ed stood still, and I wanted to keep it that way for now. "Don't fluff the blanket. Put it around your shoulders quietly."

She nodded, her chin trembling. Ed stood, the model of tolerance and good training.

"Maddie. Ed is the gentlest, calmest horse I've ever known. But I don't want the blanket to surprise him." She nodded; her gaze riveted between Ed's ears.

I, too, had to use the woodpile to mount the giant beast. Holding lines in one hand, I slipped in behind Maddie and grabbed mane with the other to balance myself. I made sure she had a good seat, then wrapped my arms around her and whispered in her ear. "Hold onto his mane like me. I promise it won't hurt him."

I watched as she grabbed a handful of Ed's mane. "Are you ready for an adventure? This will be so fun."

She nodded. "Can you make him go?"

I tickled the lines to make him pay attention. "Yes, ma'am. Back, Ed. Back." I pressed my calves against his flank. Slowly Ed took a step backward, then another and another. Once clear of the shed, I used the ring finger on my right hand to turn him. Tom had trained him and done a fine job. No need to yank the lines.

I was a bit concerned the chimney smoke would bother Ed as horses are naturally afraid of fire. An occasional crackling came from the chimney, but Ed didn't seem to care. Again, the calmness of this horse amazed me.

Ed strolled forward, Maddie relaxing with each step. It took me a while to get comfortable. I'd never ridden a draft horse. They are so much bigger than the smaller quarter horses I had always ridden.

We circled around a small hill, Ed sinking up to his knees in the snow. Our progress would be slow, but I hoped to intercept the snowcat. My plan was to drop Maddie with the SAR people in the snowcat and lead them up to the cabin with Ed.

The meadow dropped elevation slowly as it formed a shallow bowl. I wished I could figure out a way to shake the red blanket and get the snowcat's attention. But I couldn't without risking Ed balking. So, I tucked the blanket around Maddie. "You're doing great, young lady."

"This is fun. It'd be better if we were running." Spoken like a fearless kid.

"You'll get your chance to ride a horse faster. I'll take you out for a ride."

Maddie sat a little taller, eyed the snowcat, and squealed. "They see us. They're coming."

They were. Ed sensed the urgency and picked up his pace.

## Chapter Seventy-Five

Five minutes later, I stopped Ed and held him when we got off. The snowcat had changed direction and rumbled up to us. The vehicle was a huge box on tracks. I saw *Mammoth Mountain* printed across the side and under the windshield. The driver waved, and two passengers hopped out. Bundled up against the weather, a tall man with a military bearing reached out to grasp Ed's chin strap. He looked up at the little girl. "This must be Maddie. We've been looking for you." The other man and a woman stood behind him.

Clearly wary of strangers, I answered for her. "Yes, this is. She's cold and a little hungry too."

Wesley stepped out behind the tall man. "We have food and water inside the snowcat. You want to join us?"

"Wesley. Oh, I'm so glad to see you." Maddie had shrunk into my chest. I whispered in her ear. "This guy is Jake's brother and my brother-in-law. He's a pastor at my church. You can trust him, sweetheart. Just like you trust Jake and me. Okay?"

She nodded faintly and turned as Wesley reached for

her. He led her to the snowcat. Over her shoulder, he asked, "Jake?"

I smiled. "He's safe and waiting for his rescue."

Wesley had Maddie inside the snowcat in no time, seated next to the woman. With the door closed, the heater must have been on. Wesley peeled a banana for her and dug out an energy bar. She was in good hands.

The tall man let go of Ed's bridle. "I'm Lieutenant Lawrence Oswald from Mono County sheriff's office. I'm told you may need rescuing too."

"I'm fine, but my friend is in that cabin up there. He could use a ride out."

Oswald's gaze followed my finger.

"See the smoke?"

"Yes, ma'am. Hmm, looks like a chimney fire." He glanced back at me. "We had the coordinates, but none of our geo-mapping programs show a cabin out here. With the storm, we were on a fishing expedition."

"Well, I'm glad you caught us. If you'll follow Ed and me, we'll show you to your next mission." I had to get Ed's harness and the sleigh. Besides, I wanted to be sure nothing went wrong with Jake's rescue.

## Chapter Seventy-Six

We turned to the cabin. It was easy to spot because of the smoke, even though the sparkles had diminished. Jake must have run out of sawdust. We plodded along, the snowcat humming behind us.

Ed shook his head, then stopped and pawed on the snow at his knees. This wasn't normal for him. I reached to his neck, gave him a gentle pat, and encouraged him with a "good boy." I urged him forward, and he took a step. Then he moved toward the cabin but at a slower pace.

We were thirty feet away and beginning to ascend the small grade to the cabin when I heard a rumbling. It wasn't the snowcat.

Oh no. An earthquake. I slid off Ed's back, holding onto the lines, and sank into four feet of snow. The meadow undulated beneath us in a gentle motion that made me dizzy. It was like being in a boat without your sea legs. Ed didn't like it one bit. He shied and then settled as the motion faded.

Wes and Lawrence jumped out of the snowcat. "Was

that an earthquake?" Wes glanced at me and then up to the cabin. With the shriek of wood against wood, the cabin folded, dust and snow billowing upward. The metal roof clattered off to the front.

"Jake!" I tried to run but couldn't make any headway in the snow. Finally, I led Ed up to the snowcat track, stepped on the treads, and hopped on the horse. Ed made faster time than I could while the snowcat rushed past and led the way.

"Jake!" I screamed as I dismounted, dropping the lines. Wes and Lawrence were already walking the perimeter. I heard Wes calling for his brother. I pulled Lawrence's arm. "Maddie?"

He looked past me and raised a hand to the occupants of the snowcat. "She's in there with another team member. She's fine."

I heard a muffled voice, Jake's, from inside. I pointed to where I'd last seen him, somewhere near the hole.

Wes stretched out on the packed snow and poked around where the space had been. Wes called to Lawrence. "He's here, under the logs."

All I could think about was how heavy those logs were when we hauled them. "Oh my god. They'll crush him."

Wes hollered. "Jake, can you knock on the log closest to you?"

A dull thump came from beneath a log.

"Okay, bud. We'll get you out of there." Wes stood and consulted Lawrence, who walked back to the snow-cat. Then Wes turned to me. "We'll have to wait for another cat. This one can't move the logs safely."

"How long will that take?" It could be hours. Did Jake have that much time? "What do you need?"

"Lawrence is going to call for a different cat that has a

crane-type arm. Your guess is as good as mine about when the right equipment will show up. We have to lift or pull the top logs off, but the space between the rock and the cabin is too narrow."

"That's easy, Wes. Jake and I have already done it once today."

He looked at me like I'd spoken Martian.

"Look." I pointed to the huge tree branch sticking out of the remains of the roof. "Jake and I had to move logs to get Maddie and Arco out when that happened. We used Ed." I nodded toward the horse standing outside the woodshed.

Whoops, better get those lines so he doesn't step on them, scare himself, and hurt himself or someone else. I ran over, picked them up, and looped them over the branch of a nearby tree. Ed stood, patient and waiting.

"And Ed's here," I said when I returned, huffing with the exertion. "We can do this now."

Lawrence returned from the snowcat. "They said it'll be a couple of hours at the most. The rig is coming from the main lodge."

"There is another option," Wesley smiled, nodding at Ed, who nosed at the pine needles.

"What d'you mean?" Lawrence glanced from Wesley to me.

It was my turn to explain. "We've used him once already today to pull logs away from the cabin. He's capable. The only thing we need is some more rope or a cable to tie to the log."

"I can help with that." Lawrence said. "We carry chains and cables. Tell me what needs to happen."

Lawrence and I set out to look over what kind of cables he had. Within a half hour, I had Ed tacked up. Lawrence and Wesley hooked a cable around the top log.

With the two men keeping the log stable, I guided Ed. We moved it beyond the shed with the other logs.

We repeated the process twice more. When the third log jerked free, I heard Jake's voice. "I'm out." I couldn't see where he'd been. Lawrence finished controlling the log into place. I heard Wesley shouting, "He's out. He's okay." Wesley would know how worried I'd be.

As Lawrence and I unhooked the log, I heard Jake's voice sounding almost exultant. "Merry Christmas, brother."

# Chapter Seventy-Seven

A snowcat transported Jake and me to the waiting ambulance. It felt so nice to be warm, even if it was only for the half-hour ride to the ambulance. The medics did a quick check on both of us and decided we needed to be transported to the emergency room because we'd been out in the elements for so long. Clearly, they hadn't gotten the news about the cabin we'd passed the night in.

In the Mountain Meadows Resort parking lot, Wesley told me he'd arranged for Tom to get a ride on a snowmobile so he could pick up Ed. When I asked about the sleigh, he didn't know about any plans for that. I assumed Tom would stick with the original plan to haul it out after the snow melted a bit.

Maddie had already left in a separate ambulance, accompanied by the female SAR team member, to Mammoth Hospital. It was there she was to meet with her father.

Still in the parking lot, a pair of medics checked Jake

and me out. They strongly suggested we go to the hospital with them. At the cabin, he'd rolled into a cavity left by a displaced log. The remaining logs rolled over him, not onto him. While he wasn't injured in any apparent manner, the medics said the doctor wanted to look into his health further. His guardian angel worked overtime today.

An hour later and cold again, I sat on the gurney in a curtained cubicle in the ER. An aide had taken my clothes because they were still wet from the snow. She'd given me a gown with a tie in front and thin socks with treads on the bottom. I waited for a nurse, or doctor, or anyone who could spring me from this trap. Right after admission, my vitals were normal. Except I was hungry. I'd had enough water, so I wasn't dehydrated. But I was seriously hungry.

I decided to try the nurses' station to see if I could round up a can of apple juice or something for Jake and me. I wasn't sure where they'd stuck him, but I figured he'd be nearby and just as hungry.

The thin socks were good for traction. I was in no danger of slipping as I sneaked about looking for Jake. After looking in on a woman patient holding a cold pack on her eye, I was able to find Jake quickly. I didn't need to look any further. He was in the same shape I was— gowned, slippered, and hungry. "I think I know where we can find something to eat—or at least drink." I took his hand as he jumped off the gurney. We slipped down the hall toward the unoccupied nurses' station. I glanced at the entrance doors, then down the hallway. Christmas carols played softly in another part of the hospital.

But here, it looked like Jake, me, and the woman with the cold pack were the only ones around. Staff had left all the vacant curtained cubicles open but one. The curtains in the back corner were closed, but I had found Jake. I didn't feel I needed to check it. I turned back to the nurses' station.

The nurses' station was in the middle of the main corridor that comprised the emergency department. Once at the station, I found the small refrigerator. At the risk of being found out, I rifled through bottles of meds to a stack of orange, cranberry, and apple juice boxes. I took them all, handing a half dozen to Jake.

We were in the process of handing them off to each other when I heard Maddie's shout. "Mommy."

The glass entrance doors slid open, and Will Hall and his wife walked in. Maddie's mother was tall and thin, pale by any standard. She looked tired and frail, bundled in a puffy coat, her hair covered with a colorful scarf that accented her light pallor. She leaned heavily on Will's arm.

Maddie was on the far corner in a curtained-off cubicle. She swung the curtain aside. The search and rescue woman that had stayed with her from the snowcat stood in alarm. Good luck trying to control this dynamo, I laughed to myself. I pictured Maddie spying on everyone through a break in the curtains, waiting for her parents.

There was no holding back this force of nature. "Mommy. Mommy." Maddie sobbed as she ran across the room. She plunged into the weak woman, but Will held them both in a sturdy embrace. Maddie buried her face in her mother's chest, squeezing her arms around.

"Mommy, I thought I'd lost you." Maddie's words were muffled into her mother's jacket.

The woman reached around to her daughter's wild hair and smoothed it. Well, she tried to smooth it. "I believed we lost *you*."

Quietly Will spoke up, and I barely heard him over

Maddie's sobs. "I believed I was going to lose you both." Will glanced at Jake and me, standing at the nurses' station, arms full of boxed drinks. "This is the best Christmas gift ever."

# Chapter Seventy-Eight

Christmas arrived in the nick of time, pardon the pun. Jake was safe, Maddie found, and Ed was happily munching on grass hay mixed with a bit of alfalfa back in a stall at Tom and Anna's. He'd weathered the sleigh rides fine.

It was Christmas Eve, the time that kids wait for all year. At the moment, the Gibson and Murray families had no little kids to indulge, but we had plenty to celebrate. Before dinner, Libby and Cameron had stopped by for eggnog. They visited for a while, then left for dinner at Cameron's parents' house. I'd invited Kelly McSorley to stop by for pie, but he had yet to make an appearance. He was on duty, so his arrival time was unpredictable.

Anna and Mom laid out a memorable meal. Turkey and ham, mashed and sweet potatoes, green bean casserole, and a generous green salad. Parker House rolls from Layers as well as the usual array of various kinds of olives, cheeses, celery sticks, carrots, and salami filled out the rest of the dinner menu. Family, new and old, populated the table. Hosted by the Gibsons and aided by my mother, Meg Murray, the new family included Gibson son-in-law Wesley Charters's father, George, and brother, Jake. I'm sure there were fingers crossed that brother Jake would be related in a different way—soon.

Jake and Wes enthralled the table with the story of Maddie's, then Jake's rescue. Jake took the ribbing well that he got from Tom and George. Imagine, rescuing a rescuer. Then fudge ribbon cake, a family favorite, was served along with pumpkin pie for those who didn't like chocolate.

### Fudge Ribbon Cake

- 1 cup plus 2 tbs. butter, melted and divided
- 8 oz. cream cheese
- 2 ¼ cup sugar
- 1 tbs. cornstarch
- 3 eggs
- 2 tbs. plus 1 1/3 cup milk, divided
- 1 ½ tsp. vanilla extract
- 2 cups flour
- 1 tsp. salt
- 1 tsp. baking powder
- ½ tsp. baking soda
- 4 squares baking chocolate (or 12 tbs. cocoa plus 4 tbs. butter)

For the cream cheese ribbon:

Cream 2 tbs. of softened butter with cream cheese, ¼ cup sugar, and cornstarch. Add in 1 egg, 2 tbs. milk, and ½ tsp. vanilla. Beat until smooth and creamy (at high speed). Set aside.

For the chocolate cake:

Combine 2 cups of flour with 2 cups of sugar, salt, baking

*powder, and baking soda in a large mixing bowl. Add in ½ cup*
*butter, 1 cup milk, 2 eggs, chocolate, and 1 tsp. vanilla. Beat*
*for 1 minute. Place half of the chocolate batter in the bottom*
*of a greased pan. Add cream cheese mixture. Add the rest of*
*the batter. Bake at 350 degrees in a 9x13-inch cake pan*
*(greased and floured) for 50-60 minutes. Use a toothpick to*
*test.*

*Frost the cake with a chocolate fudge frosting:*

- *¼ cup milk*
- *¼ cup butter, softened*
- *1 cup chocolate chips (semi-sweet)*
- *1 tsp. vanilla*
- *1 to 1 ½ cups powdered sugar*

*Combine the milk and butter in a saucepan. Bring to a boil and*
*remove from heat. Pour in the chocolate chips, vanilla, and 1 cup*
*powdered sugar. Beat until combined. If the frosting seems too*
*thin, add up to ½ cup more of powdered sugar. When the cake is*
*evenly cool, spread the frosting over it. Store your leftovers in the*
*fridge.*

Kelly almost missed the pie. He rang the doorbell just
as the first piece of cake was set before Tom. After hearty
Christmas greetings, Wesley and Jake scooted their
chairs over for Kelly to squeeze in at the table.

Jake addressed Kelly. "You almost missed your pie,
big guy. Been busy?"

Kelly chewed until he could talk without spitting out
his pie. "Not really. Tonight's more about stopping by
places that could use a smiling face." He grinned at his
private joke. "I had a few gifts for Santa to give out."

"Like maybe you tore up that speeding ticket you

gave Mark last month?" Tom squinted at Mark across the table. Mark shook his head at the reminder.

Kelly's hands flew up with innocence. "It wasn't me. A case of mistaken identity. Must've been the highway patrol."

Mom poured a cup of coffee for Kelly and set it in front of him. "How's the search for Norman Escher's murderer going?"

The table fell silent. This was important information for this family. We all had felt the repercussions of Norman's actions. His murder made it doubly intriguing.

Kelly looked at Jake. "Okay to spill it?" The actual murder had taken place in Bishop, Jake's soon-to-be jurisdiction.

"Now they know that you know everyone at this table would beat you to a pulp if you didn't tell." Jake snorted a laugh then his cheerfulness faded. This was more serious business, and Jake was soon to be the PD chief. "Besides this being BPD's case, it is also a joint effort between several agencies."

Kelly stirred sugar and cream into his coffee. He finished the last bite of his pie and pushed the plate away. He scanned the faces at the table. "Sarah's audio file set the whole thing in motion. Good thinking, by the way." He tipped his coffee mug to me. "With the deposit slips, receipts, and invoices that were recovered at the pawnshop, the Los Angeles County sheriff has served a search warrant at Anchorman Holdings in Lancaster. Without getting into detail here, their detectives were able to unravel a web of couriers like Norman Escher. He was like a mule, being used to launder big money from a large syndicate. They were trying a new money laundering method, but it turned out to be more effort than it was worth. The business part of it is complicated, but

LASO is zeroing in on the main company and its boss. It's interesting to note that the detectives were able to identify the guy you called Muscles as Igor Dulik. Their organized crime unit was familiar with him. They knew where to find him and arrested him. He's been charged with homicide due to Sarah's recording, but they said there were a few more open homicides they wanted to connect to him." He glanced at me. "You might have to go down south to testify in court."

Tom looked at me. "Justice well served. Great work, Sarah." He lifted a coffee cup in a toast. The table raised their glasses and coffee cups to me, but my eyes, and my heart, were on Jake and his lopsided grin.

# Chapter Seventy-Nine

K elly left soon after dessert, saying he had another stop to make. Coffee and brandy were served in the living room. After we finished putting all the leftovers and the dishes away, Anna, Mark, and I joined the family for Christmas gift-opening. The requisite sweaters, ties, and blenders were unwrapped, ogled over, and put away. The joy was not in the presents but the delight in having a family with whom to share it all. This was a memorable Christmas.

For some, it was a holiday without a loved one. More than Wesley, Tom and Anna missed Melody. Although I hadn't attended ten Christmases with my family, this one was particularly tough without her. As I looked around the room, I saw a teary eye every now and then. But now was the time for new family too. George and Jake were additions, and my family embraced them both.

With the fresh-cut tree in the corner, lights twinkling and ornaments sparkling, I was sure the scene would inspire a modern-day Norman Rockwell portrait. Finally, Mom began scooping up wrapping paper and ribbons, saving what she could reuse, and tossing the rest in the garbage. The evening was winding down.

George caught my eye and nodded to the sunroom. With more than a little trepidation, I followed. The last two days' adventure drained my energy. I'm sure Jake wanted to get back to Wesley's and grab some pillow time.

George motioned for me to sit down across from him. He cleared his throat and began. "This isn't easy for me, Sarah. I've never been known for my kind sentiments. But I feel I owe you an apology."

"George, there's no need. Let's just forget…"

"No." He insisted, looking at his feet. "No, I have to make this right." His lips clamped together like he hated the words coming out of them. "You and Kristin are different in a lot of ways. But Jake and Wesley's story about you is factual. I can tell. Jake doesn't exaggerate, neither does Wes. I was wrong about you. Your strength, courage, and moxie have saved not only that little girl, but Jake too."

"I'm sure that…"

"No. Don't spit out any false modesty to me. I see right through you. You're a hero." He shook his head. I guessed he might have reevaluated how wrong his earlier opinion of me had been. "I can't even speculate what Kristin would've done in a similar situation." He finally looked up at me with deep sadness. "We'll never know."

I couldn't think of what to say to that. The man had obviously felt strongly about his daughter-in-law. Maybe he was just now admitting that she was gone. Maybe he was enveloping himself in the shroud of grief when a person has lost a loved one. Maybe there was a chance he'd accept me.

"I'm sorry for the loss of your daughter-in-law. I

know Jake loved her dearly and I can see you did too. I know I cannot replace her. I wouldn't even try."

He nodded, looking away. "Hmm."

"Maybe we can start over."

He frowned and nodded once.

I waited for him to comment, but Wesley called out, "Jake and Dad, time to leave these fine people so they can be asleep when Santa arrives." He whistled for Arco, who trotted past Jake and out the door.

The Charters family made for their car. Jake lingered on the front porch long enough for his lips to brush across mine. He traced my jawline and whispered, "I'll see you for brunch tomorrow at your house. I'll have something for you."

# Chapter Eighty

Christmas morning was almost like it had been when I was a child. It was just the three of us. The exception was that our gift-giving wasn't the focus of the day as it was when I was young. Still, it was wonderful to see the surprise on Dad's face when he unwrapped a GoSky spotting scope for wildlife viewing with a tripod and carrying bag.

Mom was equally astonished at a cooking class gift certificate from a local shop called Mary Anne's Kitchen Store. She immediately began the debate about which class she would take—Asian, Mexican, or Mediterranean cuisine. I loved making these two happy.

They each gifted me with something special as well. Dad got me a year-long roadside assistance insurance. Given Bishop's remote location, this was something I hoped I'd never have to use. But if I had to, it was great protection. There were miles and miles between tow trucks in Inyo County, and if my new car broke down, I'd need help. Mom gave me a luxurious sky-blue cashmere sweater. I couldn't wait to put it on. I put my gift for Jake under the tree, my mind casting ideas about what he planned to give me.

After hugs and gift wrap pick-up, Mom took a shower while I started the breakfast casseroles. When she finished, she'd take over, and I'd have my shower. I put off wearing my new sweater until after we cooked and donned my usual off-work uniform—jeans and a T-shirt.

Anna showed up early to help. I handed over my apron and took Rusty outside. The morning sky was cloudless, the air crisp and bright with sunlight. One would never know that yesterday there had been a storm fewer than forty miles and twenty-four hours away. An involuntary shudder went through me when I remembered the dangers we'd faced and how cold it had been. We were lucky we'd survived the storm. Meteorologists called it the storm of the decade. Vehicles were stuck on Highway 395 from south of Bishop to north of June Lake. The highway patrol and road departments closed the road to clear snow and cars. Most of the highway had been plowed and was open by now. The sun would melt the little snow left in Bishop.

The small shaker that finished off wrecking the cabin came in at a mere 3.5 on the Richter scale. Barely a shelf emptier.

It was late morning when our company arrived. Tom came in, gripping his coffee travel mug. He managed a quick kiss on Anna's cheek as she scurried around Mom's kitchen, going from one project to another. He made Mark's apologies. Their son had committed to spend the day with his buddy, Pete Irving. Mom took the news amiably, without any sign of her previous misgivings about Mark.

The doorbell rang then The door flew open without being answered. Wesley hollered, "Hallo, the house," when he and George strolled in, one holding a bottle of sparkling cider and the other with wine. Jake followed, and Arco sauntered beside him.

Rusty darted past Arco, who whirled around and followed. Trotting out behind them, Jake said, "I've got the dogs."

A minute later, Jake returned, beaming. "Guess who just dropped by."

Maddie and her father trailed in. Maddie jogged across the room to give me a hug while Will Hall stood apologizing. "I'm sorry, you guys. I know it's an intrusion on Christmas Day, but we just wanted to stop by and say thank you."

The moms dropped their kitchen work and enveloped them with hugs. Tom and Dad shook Will's hand when he'd disentangled himself from the women. Beside me, Maddie chattered about the ambulance ride as if that had been the highlight of her adventure.

"Is your mom at home?"

Maddie's generous curls shook as she nodded. "Her sister is here for Christmas, and she's with her now, so we could visit you. She's a nurse." Maddie looked so proud of her auntie that I hated to ask. My gaze met Will. "And your grandfather, Norman?"

Maddie got serious, and her father wrapped his hands around her shoulders. She was more serious than an eleven-year-old girl needs to be. She'd faced tragedies that adults couldn't cope with. I hated to break the spell of gratitude that these two people spread. "Grandpa passed away. He died trying to protect me." She looked up at her father, then back to me. "Dad said I never did anything wrong, that I shouldn't blame myself." A tear rolled down her cheek. "A lot of kids in my class say their parents don't care about them. I know different. I know who loves me."

I had to clear my throat to speak. "Yes, Maddie. You are loved. Just wait until your dad tells you about all the things the people in this town did to find you. People you don't even know came out and searched the desert, abandoned buildings, and a lot of other places."

"Dad said you were the one who got the search going."

"Oh no. It wasn't me. It was your teacher, Mister Gallagher. I got a phone call from a friend who introduced me to Mister Gallagher from your school. He told me you were missing and gave me enough information to start searching for you."

Will flashed a grateful smile and said, "Then we'll have to say thank you to him too. But we still believe no one could have found Maddie without you and Jake."

I waved the compliment aside. I've never been good with accolades, whether deserved or not. But I was happy to see these two on the most meaningful day of the year. I was happy Maddie got to be home with her mother and father.

After graciously refusing casseroles and coffee, Will and Maddie left, saying one last thank you. I felt satisfied that I'd done my best to find Maddie and get her home for Christmas, even if it was without her grandfather.

We closed the door behind the Halls, and the Gibsons, Murrays, and the Charters sat down for our Christmas breakfast. The casseroles were family favorites, Brunch Eggs and French Toast Casserole. Bacon, sausage, and scrambled eggs with a fresh fruit salad rounded out the menu. Christmas cookies came out afterward with the dessert leftovers from last night.

My favorite cookies were the Russian Tea Cakes and the Chocolate Crinkle Cookies.

### Russian Tea Cakes

- ½ cup powdered sugar
- 1 cup unsalted butter, softened
- 1 tsp. vanilla extract

Add:

- 2 ¼ cup flour
- ¾ cup finely chopped walnuts

Whisk flour and 6 tbs. of powdered sugar together in separate bowl. Add the butter mixture and stir until just blended. Add walnuts and mix until incorporated; mixture may be crumbly.

Form into 1-inch balls and place them 2 inches apart on ungreased cookie sheets. Bake in a preheated oven of 350 degrees until the edges are golden brown (about 12 minutes). Remove from the oven and transfer to a wire rack to cool for 15 minutes. Place remaining powdered sugar in a small bowl and roll cooled cookies in it once or twice.

### Chocolate Crinkle Cookies

- ½ cup vegetable oil
- 2 squares unsweetened chocolate, melted
- 2 cups sugar
- 4 eggs
- 2 tsp. vanilla
- ½ tsp. salt

- *2 cups sifted flour*
- *2 tsp. baking powder*
- *1 cup powdered sugar*

*Mix oil, chocolate, and sugar together. Blend in one egg at a time until well-mixed. Add vanilla. Sir in salt, flour, and baking powder. Chill for several hours or overnight. Heat oven to 350 degrees. Drop teaspoons of dough into the powdered sugar, rolling them around and shaping them into balls. Place them 2 inches apart on a greased baking sheet. Bake for 10 to 12 minutes.*

Ninety minutes later, the dads and I had leftovers put away and the dishes done. The last of the mulled cider and coffee had been drunk. With the table cleared, Dad brought out a cribbage board which drew Tom, Wesley, and George. Mom and Anna sat in companionable silence, regrouping from two days of frantic preparation. Christmas was always a high-energy event, but this year, even more so. No one could guess when Jake and I would be found, so this Christmas stayed fluid, ready to be celebrated whenever we got home. The family gratitude meter was off the chart.

I finished wiping down the kitchen counter and felt a hand on my shoulder. Jake.

I turned to see his soft brown eyes and gentle smile. "Would you like to go for a walk with Arco and me?"

# Chapter Eighty-One

We walked slowly, savoring the peaceful afternoon. Periodically, someone we knew would drive by and wave. We'd wave back, and I felt the deepest sense of satisfaction I had felt in months, maybe years. Rusty had to come when he saw Arco leashed up. The two had become dear companions, frolicking in the remnants of fall leaves and chasing toys. We walked McLaren Lane to Mountain View Drive and across West Line. We both seemed to be heading to Mumy Lane without exchanging words.

Once on Mumy Lane, we unleashed the dogs. Rusty took off down the rough road, his tongue lolling out the side of his mouth when he looked back for Arco. Arco wasn't too far behind, but he didn't move quite as fast as Rusty. Jake mentioned Arco's arthritis got worse in the winter.

We got to the first creek crossing on Mumy Lane—North Fork Bishop Creek—a tired fence on each side of the roadway marked the creek flowing underneath. One hundred yards further was South Fork Bishop Creek, but we stopped here. We watched the early snowmelt rushing over the rocks, hissing with power, and frothing with energy. "Hard to believe this was all a blizzard just yesterday."

Jake exhaled. "You were right when you said living here wasn't like living in the 'burbs."

"I was gone long enough that Dad had to remind me, but yeah. It's very elemental. The land isn't very forgiving." I turned to face him. "I hope you're going to be happy here. I know you'll miss Petaluma but having Wes and your father here should help."

"And you." His index finger tipped my chin upward to look into his eyes. "Having you here is crucial to my happiness."

His lips brushed mine in the tiniest kiss. "Jake," I whispered. So many thoughts ran through my mind. Would he be happy here? Would he be happy with me? What about the job? Bishop PD is a much smaller agency than Petaluma PD. Would it satisfy him?

"Sarah." His hand dropped to grasp both of mine. Rusty yapped in the distance, but it barely registered. "I never believed I could fall in love again after losing Kristin. My heart broke, and I locked it away to keep it from hurting any more. That all ended the night I met you in the sheriff's substation."

His lopsided grin took my breath away. I was glad he didn't ask for anything from me at this point because I had no words to express how I felt.

"I knew I was in trouble when you told me who to look at as a suspect for your cousin's murder. You were a force to be reckoned with then. If I could admit this without getting punched, I'd say you're even tougher now."

"Now you're going to get punched." I raised my arm

in a mock threat, and my hand found the back of his neck. I pushed him toward me for another kiss, this one lengthier than the last. I held my breath, and my heart pounded in my ears.

"Sarah, I can't wait any longer. I cannot imagine going through life without you. You bring such excitement and joy into my life. It's like I was living in black and white. Meeting you has opened the door to a life of color. I don't want to waste another minute without a commitment from you." He reached into his jeans pocket and went down on one knee on the rough asphalt. In his fingers was a stunning antique solitaire diamond ring in a gold setting with filigree engravings. "Sarah, will you marry me?"

"Yes, Jake. Yes." My heart thumped in my chest so loud I was sure he could hear it. As if they knew, Arco and Rusty charged at us, circling and barking. This is what life with Jake would be like. Exciting.

I had a moment to question myself. "Wait. Are you sure? I can't promise I won't interfere in an investigation. People come to me, Jake."

"I know, Sarah. I know that people trust you. People know you'll do what you can to help. That's something that I love about you. I wouldn't change it if I could."

"I'll try not to get into trouble." My voice held a tiny spark of remorse. I knew I couldn't promise that I'd stay away. This was the best I could do.

"Sarah. Your snooping is one thing I've learned to appreciate in you. You have great instincts, as good as any cop I've known. Better than some." His wry smile told me all I needed to know. "I trust you. You're sensible enough not to do anything stupid or unwarranted."

Sometimes I wondered about that myself, but he

sounded convinced. One hurdle down. Now for the second one. "What about your father, Jake? Even though he apologized, he's made it clear that he doesn't care for me. I'll never compare to his image of Kristin."

His smile warmed me as a cold gust of wind blew past us. "You don't have to. He's figured out that you're something special. Where do you think I got this ring?"

"Your father? But he divorced both his wives."

Jake nodded. "At the end, my mother gave this ring back to him. It was his mother's, and she wanted it to stay in the family. Mom gave it to him so one of his sons could use it." Of all the Christmas magic I'd experienced, all I could've imagined, none could compete with this.

# Chapter Eighty-Two

Rusty and Arco blasted through the door at the McLaren house, like eager children bursting with news. They should've been tired by now. We'd walked over two miles.

The cribbage gang was still at the table, and Mom and Anna were in the sunroom. I called the ladies out, and Jake got the attention of the cribbage players. I stood next to Jake, holding his hand as he called the crowd to attention. Laughing at each other, they called out bets as to who would score first. "You can get back to your game in a minute. Sarah and I have something important to tell you."

That got their attention. The stark silence bordered on a surprise. Jake cleared his throat. "I have asked Sarah to marry me, and she has accepted."

The room erupted with congratulations, embraces, and much merriment. "Now Jake will be a genuine member of the family, not just a shirttail relative, like me." George cackled as he made his way through the crowd to me.

He nodded to the room. "If you all will excuse the heroine and me, I have something to tell her. He grasped my hand and led me into the sunroom, where we were alone. He'd sounded like he'd buried the hard feelings. He still made me nervous.

"George."

"Sarah," he said, grasping my elbows. "Can you forgive an old man's anger?" He stared into my eyes. "I've had my son close by for four years now, and the idea of sharing him has put me into a funk."

Trying to build on the positive, I offered my thoughts. "Of course, I understand your anger. It seems natural. And now you're in Bishop, you'll have both your boys nearby."

His face lined with disapproval. "Yeah, a preacher and a cop."

"Most parents would be proud. They're both wonderful men."

"Yes." His deep sigh took a moment. "I have to agree. But it was mostly their mothers who raised them. I had the good taste to pick women who turned out to be good mothers." He took my hand, turning it to see the engagement ring. "This ring sitting on Jake's wife's finger was important to Jake's mother."

"What about Kristin? Why didn't she have the ring?"

George cocked his head sideways. "I asked Barbara— that was Jake's mother's name. I asked her that, you know. She never really answered. I got the feeling she didn't admire Kristin like I did." Then he shrugged. "Maybe she didn't want to part with it. Anyway, just before she passed, she called me in to give this to me. By then, Kristin was already gone."

I was bewildered. Words didn't come as I considered

that Jake's beloved Kristin didn't have his grandmother's ring. But I did.

Wesley stepped into the room, leaned down to pet Rusty and eyed his father. "Dad, the folks have something to say. They want you to hear it, but it's for Sarah —and Jake too." He stepped back, waiting for us to pass. "Shall we?"

I followed George into the living room. Everyone was sitting except for Jake. His gaze met mine, and he shrugged. This sounded important. What could it mean?

# Chapter Eighty-Three

Wesley took up a position standing in front of the gaily decorated fireplace. Christmas cards sent to the family from all over the west hung above the mantle. The mantle itself cloaked with evergreen boughs that fragranced the warm ambiance inside. Mom and Dad sat in their usual places with Tom and Anna on the sofa. Dad had moved in a comfortable chair for George. As soon as he sat, Wesley began.

"Sarah, except for your dad's optometry practice, our families have done business together for a long time. Beyond cattle and horse drives with and without tourists, we've decided to branch out. We now have an opportunity to go in together on a commercial enterprise."

Jake asked, "Doing what?"

"Just wait until I get my speech out." Wesley's voice was shaky. He wasn't used to talking for the families. This must be big. He was the sole owner of Layers, so I assumed it had something to do with the bakery. "Judith Bateau has offered us the purchase of Boulangerie for a third of what it is worth. She wants a quick sale in cash.

The three of our families can swing the financial part of it."

"Wait. What?" Surprise fluttered in my brain. "Wesley, a few months ago, you were renegotiating your rent. How could you make enough to be the third partner?"

A patient smile spread across his lips. "You, Sarah. You funneled all the Layers profits to me. Even after taking a percentage for Better Off Baking, you put me in the black, coz. I don't really have that many expenses."

I dropped to a chair. Surprise was an understatement. I glanced at Jake, then back to Wes. Judging by the look on his face, this was news to Jake too. He asked, "But who's going to run Layers while you're working at Boulangerie?"

"We've decided one of our stipulations for this sale is that you should be in charge of both bakeries."

Holy cow. "Have you purchased it yet?" My voice sounded like a croak.

Dad answered. "It's in escrow. If you decide against this, we'll look for someone else, but truthfully, the luster will have gone off the sale."

I felt heat rising in my face. I was on the spot. "But I'm not a baker. Besides, I have a job with the courts waiting for me in January." I loved going to court each day, listening to sharp attorneys and sharper jurists. But that was LA, and this is Inyo County. There was a significant difference in the job description too. With visions of getting coffee for the judges, I'd been concerned about that but pushed it aside.

Dad's answer was short. "You'd have to let that go."

Tom piped up. "We figured out the salary. We could pay the same as the court job. And as far as you not being a baker, with the crew you've assembled at Layers, you don't have to be. You're a manager, good with employees and the public. Heck, Paula at the chamber has been after me to get you on board with them."

"Keeping your continuity with BOB will benefit the students. And you could take all the time off you need." Mom had her hopeful face on. The one she had on eleven years ago when she told me I didn't have to marry Blaine if I didn't want to.

The opportunity sounded so attractive, but this would be a significant life change. I'd loved working with Libby—who'd be leaving soon—and Charlie, Marie, Javier, and Rosalyn. Even Austin was pitching in on the clock. Layers gave me freedom and creativity that court reporting didn't. I may not bake, but I sure can enable those who do. "Let me talk this over with Jake."

Jake and I went into the sunroom. I pulled out a sheet of paper and listed all the pros, which filled half the page, one of them being the ease of taking time off for maternity leave should the situation arise. Oh my. That was exciting, and I saw a gleam in his eyes.

Then the cons. Only one con came to mind. I loved my court job. Then it seemed simple. Jake wrapped his arms around me. "Whatever you want to do is the answer. I'll be beside you, whichever career you choose."

We kissed on it and returned to the living room.

"Mom, Dad, Tom and Anna, and Wesley. It's a deal!"

## If you liked this, you may also enjoy: Home is Where You Are

### RAFTER O RANCH BOOK ONE BY NATALIE BRIGHT AND DENISE F. MCALLISTER

*They say home is where the heart is...*

But what if that home is located on barren, unforgiving land with nothing but giant animals, wind, and God-given dirt?

When Nathan Olsen brings his wife, Indya, and their 18-month-old son home to Rafter O Ranch for his little brother's wedding, he only plans to be there for a few days. He didn't prepare himself for the possibility that being home with family again would stir up longings for his family's ranch and their way of life—a lifestyle that only a rancher with generations of family who worked the land could understand.

But when the wedding they're visiting for veers toward disaster and ends with them staying for good, can their marriage survive the turmoil that change too-often brings?

With Nathan and Indya at odds, Indya discovers a warm and welcoming family who accepts her—a worldly island girl—into their close-knit group. But she can't shake the feeling that comradery isn't enough...and begins to worry that this stark and barren landscape will never become a place she loves as much as her beloved Santa Fe.

When the heart isn't where it wants to be, can a marriage survive?

*Rafter O is set in the same Texas town as Wild Cow Ranch. Pick up your copy today and jump into the pages of a picturesque cattle ranch, inhabited by endearing and unforgettable characters.*

***AVAILABLE NOW***